AVA'S REVENGE

AN UNBOUNDED NOVELLA

Books by Teyla Branton

Unbounded Novels
The Change
The Cure
The Escape
The Reckoning
The Takeover

Unbounded Novellas
Ava's Revenge
Mortal Brother
Lethal Engagement
Set Ablaze

Colony Six
Sketches

Under the Name Rachel Branton

Lily's House
House Without Lies
Tell Me No Lies
Your Eyes Don't Lie
Hearts Never Lie

Noble Hearts
Royal Quest
Royal Dance

AN UNBOUNDED NOVELLA

TEYLA BRANTON

This is a work of fiction, and the views expressed herein are the sole responsibility of the author. Likewise, certain characters, places, and incidents are the product of the author's imagination, and any resemblance to actual persons, living or dead, or actual events or locales, is entirely coincidental.

Ava's Revenge (An Unbounded Novella)

Published by White Star Press
P.O. Box 353
American Fork, Utah 84003

Copyright © 2014 by Nunes Entertainment, LLC
Cover design copyright © 2014 by White Star Press

All rights reserved. No part of this book may be scanned, uploaded, reproduced, distributed, or transmitted in any form or by any means whatsoever without written permission from the author, except in the case of brief quotations embodied in critical articles and reviews. Thank you for supporting the author's rights.

Printed in the United States of America
ISBN: 978-1-939203-55-7
Year of first printing: 2014

To my readers who have enjoyed the Unbounded series
and wanted to know more about the characters.

PART ONE

June 1745 - Near Williamsburg, Virginia

Ava's Change

CHAPTER 1

SIMON WAS IN A BLACK MOOD, THE KIND THAT EVEN AFTER thirteen years of marriage brought terror to my heart and made me want to flee. I had almost run away a year ago, but I couldn't do that now because of Hannah. I couldn't risk her.

I could feel him coming, imagined slights and impotent frustration clinging to him like sticky gray cobwebs. I felt the darkness as if I could see into his mind, as if I were a part of him.

He was late and dinner had long since cooled, despite my moving it on and off the heat for the past two hours. I hurried to stoke the dying fire, swinging the kettle back over the flames, praying it would reheat quickly. Simon had never been content with the customary cold leftovers from the larger afternoon meal but required all his food served hot. Though I'd originally made the roast in the oven built inside the fireplace, today I had reheated the meat in the kettle, nearly burning it when he didn't appear on time.

Stepping to the other side of the hearth, I peered out the window of our three-bedroom house—a house larger than those of our neighbors. Solid on the outside but reeking putrefaction on the inside. Sure enough, Simon was coming up the dirt road that led to our main fields, riding Old Bob. Simon's face was his normal red, and his thick, aging, slouch-shouldered body didn't appear any more tense than usual, yet the dark emotion remained lodged in my heart. Clearly, his planned discussion with our neighbor about our troublesome cow hadn't gone well.

Around his body was a glow I had been seeing around everyone since before Hannah's birth. Always the same white color—like twenty candles framing the body. I didn't know what it was, but every living thing had it, even animals and insects, except these were muted compared with the brighter human auras. It could be quite distracting at town council or in a church meeting, but for the most part I found it comforting, especially with Hannah. There was no glow around the deceased.

A sound stilled my heart. "Oh, no," I whispered. "Let me get him taken care of first." Because three-month-old Hannah knew nothing about our world and how it worked. Nothing about her father.

"Shush, my sweet." I scooped up the baby, thinking hard. I could take her to the woodshed, where her cries wouldn't be heard. I'd done it before, rescuing her as soon as possible, her face red and her fists clenched in indignation at being ignored. I would pay the price for not being in the house when he came home, but that would be preferable to his noticing Hannah.

Desperation clogged my throat. I'd lost too many babies. The first had been a boy, in my womb less than five months. Simon had cried real tears that day, his worn face sorrowful. I'd been eighteen and I'd believed the tears. Almost, I'd forgiven him.

The second baby I miscarried six months into the pregnancy, a little girl. Simon hadn't wept over her small corpse or apologized for hitting me, and that was when I began to suspect the depths of his depravation. The third baby I lost at two months after Simon kicked me in the stomach, and the fourth at five after he slammed me into the wall and locked me up for three days without food. Afterwards, Simon had been angry because I had lost another boy. He'd raped me that very evening in the effort to start another.

But that was it. No more babies. Not for me. No more victims for Simon. As the years went on, I was just Ava O'Hare Brumbaugh, the barren woman with the poor, hard-working husband, who really couldn't be blamed for stepping out at the brothel given his hardships.

Not that his attempt at showing his manhood protected me from his advances. Because he still wanted a son. I was just as determined not to give him one, so I took the herbs that women only talked about behind closed doors when their husbands and children couldn't hear. Just in case my body decided to heal.

Last year, at thirty, I discovered I was expecting again despite the prevention. Given the low life expectancy in Virginia and my volatile relationship with Simon, I was surprised I'd lived that long.

Hannah had fallen back to sleep, turning her lips toward my breast and making sucking motions, her bottom lip disappearing inside her mouth as she nursed in her dream. "Good girl," I murmured. "Please stay asleep." I stroked her soft cheek. Just once and only briefly. She was due for a feeding soon, but I couldn't have her awaken now, not with Simon in that foul mood. Unfortunately, Hannah was a fussy baby, and though I had ample milk, every day it was an increasing effort to keep her quiet.

To deepen her slumber, I held her as long as I dared. As Simon's boots sounded against the steps, I slipped her into the little cradle that lay inside the large corner cupboard where I had once kept cooking supplies.

Untucking my skirt from my underclothes where I'd put it to prevent it from catching fire, I hurried back to the fireplace.

I wasn't fast enough.

Simon's eyes pinned me as I bent to check the food, then strayed toward the cupboard, his eyes narrowing with the jealousy he showed toward anything that took my attention from him. Fury emanated from his body as prominently as the stench of his sweat.

I forced my jaw to unclench. "Good evening, Simon. How was your day? Dinner's hot and ready." This last was a lie, or maybe a desperate hope.

His eyes left the cupboard, and I nearly gave a sigh of relief, the knot in my stomach lessening slightly. "Rotten," he muttered. "Imbeciles. Barker and the rest. He had three of the others there to witness his demands for payment. It ain't my fault his old fences can't keep out my livestock. He even had the gall to ask me to fix his fence."

He looked at me expectantly, so I shook my head in commiseration. "What did you tell him?"

The potatoes and carrots were ready, and the new butter and the freshly baked bread I had struggled over all day would please him, but the meat wouldn't be as hot as he liked. I should have kept it warm, no matter his complaints about the wasted fuel. He could afford it, despite the setbacks he'd experienced lately with the crops.

Simon pulled out a chair and sat at the table, cursing under his breath as he removed his boots and tossed them by the door where I'd have to remove the caked mud later. "I told him he owes *me* for treating the cow for bloating."

I suspected that Simon had let our cow into Barker's field, or at least starved her into desperation so she would break through the fence. She was older and after the summer would become our meat for the winter. Fattening her up on Barker's grain would mean better eating for us.

Or for Simon. These days I had no appetite—a good thing because Simon seemed to begrudge anything that went into my mouth. That I hadn't lost weight or felt weak, I chalked up to a miracle.

Maybe I can find a way to leave with Hannah. He might not find us. I'd been saving every bit of money I could, but it wasn't enough to get us very far. Not yet. Simon was careful with what he gave me, and the only money I had was what I earned from my needlework for Mrs. Adamson. That tiny nest egg and the hope it represented—and sweet Hannah, of course—were the only things keeping me alive.

Because if we didn't go far enough, I knew he would find me. And he'd have help. Simon was a contributing member of our society, if not a friendly one, and most of our neighbors and acquaintances would work together to return a runaway wife. I belonged to him like the chickens or the cows.

He was proud of me in his own way. My face maintained much of my youthful beauty, my blond hair was long and lustrous, and I didn't carry extra pounds. The scars he'd given me over the years had disappeared, and even the deep bruises he now gave me faded overnight. I worked hard and needed little sleep. As long as I didn't linger too long with any of the local farmers or their sons, he was willing to take me out to church or other town functions and show me off. He even endured Hannah's presence during the outings because she represented his prowess of fathering a child.

No, the only way Simon would let me leave was in a pine box.

Like his first wife.

Until Hannah arrived, I had begun to think of the first Mistress Brumbaugh as the lucky one.

"Well?" Simon looked at me expectantly.

I swept up a plate, but instead of going to the stove, I approached him, my mind scrabbling to find a delay so the meat could heat thoroughly. "Maybe we can go for a walk this evening. Would you like that?"

He studied me, his face turning a deeper shade of red. Simon wasn't an ugly man, but there was nothing remarkable about him. His height was average, or perhaps slightly less so. He was wide and his arms thick, but his strength was also average by comparison. He looked no more or less worn than any of the other wrinkled, leather-faced men who spent their entire lives toiling under the sun.

Simon's very averageness might have fueled his ever-present anger. Maybe if he'd been taller, he would have been more confident and not so quick to take offense. If he'd been stronger, he might not have needed to prove his domination over me. If his eyes had been more compelling or his face less red, perhaps he wouldn't regard my every interaction with other men as flirting. If he'd been wealthy, instead of just slightly better off than the rest of our neighbors, or if we lived in one of the big, fancy houses in town and he was a doctor or politician instead of a farmer, maybe everything would have been different.

I didn't really believe that.

His hands fisted on the table. "Someone you want to see?" His muddy eyes felt like the cigars he'd once burned into my skin. Scars that had also disappeared—at least on the outside.

"No. You had a hard day. A stroll might help you relax, that's all."

"I'm tired. I just want my dinner. Bring it."

No more delay. Praying the flames had done their job, I glided to the fireplace, my movements seemingly unreal, a dream. I cut the bread on the hearth first, as slowly as I dared, and then filled his plate.

As I set it down on the table in front of him, his hand whipped out and gripped my breast. The knot in my stomach quadrupled in that instant. "I know what you can do to relax me," he said, squeezing tighter.

I wanted to vomit. I wanted to jerk away or tell him he was hurting me, but I knew from experience that would only make it worse.

His hand moved down to my stomach and back up again, rubbing and squeezing. "You like that, don't ya? Yeah, you live for it. I know you do." He chuckled and released me, his hand going for the knife. He sliced off a chunk of meat. "I got a few new things in mind tonight. To relax me, as you say." He chuckled as if we shared some kind of special joke. "I got more of that tranquility potion. Remember the one from a couple years back? You'll take it after you clean up dinner."

For a man who had never shown an ounce of creativity

in other areas, he knew all sorts of depravity in the bedroom—or living room, or kitchen, or barn—things that I had never dreamed existed in my girlish fantasies of married life. The idea of taking his potion, bought from some traveling snake oil salesman, frightened me beyond belief. It brought complete immobility, made me an observer to whatever indignities he would subject me to. And it would last for hours. What if Hannah needed me?

Simon had been forty when we married, just weeks short of my eighteenth birthday. At the time, I was nearly a spinster in the eyes of my parents, who had given me away like a foal to a new master. After the first year of being sadistically raped by Simon, I'd stopped talking to my parents. They should have been able to see behind the face he showed the world, the life he kept just for me in the privacy of our home. I knew it was a man's right to keep his woman in place, but that wasn't the relationship I'd dreamed about. Or planned with my first and only love, Gabriel, who at sixteen had been too young and penniless to prevent my fate as Mrs. Brumbaugh.

Maybe it was my double black eyes or the choke marks around my throat, but after losing baby number four, my widowed father had finally taken my side, realizing far too late what he had condemned me to. For my father, it was no longer the broken arm, the black eyes, or the bruises that could be explained as a man keeping his spirited young wife under control, but the slaughter of his posterity—the future.

I didn't let myself believe it stemmed from love. That was too dangerous.

He'd confronted Simon, and they'd fought. A year later my father was dead, still suffering from the leg injury he'd earned that day. His farm passed to Simon. I didn't mourn my father. I was nothing more than a corpse myself, unable to feel anything but fear. Until Hannah.

Simon took a bite of food and grunted with enjoyment. I moved to get myself a plate with a thin slice of meat and only two small pieces of potatoes. He liked my company so he could brag about the day, and he would be angry if I didn't eat or if I ate too much.

"I'm planting the south field next week," he said. "You'll bring out our food. I'm hiring Wilson's boys to help."

A rustling from the cupboard clogged my response in my throat, but there was no cry, so Hannah was probably just moving in her sleep.

I still didn't know how she'd happened, but the moment I'd realized I was expecting, I'd talked nonstop about the son Simon would have and what people would say. How he'd have someone to bestow his legacy upon. I'd made sure plenty of witnesses were at the birth, and when it was a daughter—after the fear subsided—I was fiercely glad. A daughter I might be able to protect from his anger. A daughter wouldn't follow in her father's footsteps.

But whenever he had to hire other men's sons, he remembered that Hannah wasn't the heir I'd promised.

He'd never forgiven me for what he thought of as my betrayal.

"I'll do that," I said. It'd actually be nice to cook for someone who might appreciate the effort.

Simon took a second bite of meat, and this time his face furrowed. He swallowed and took another mouthful. This one he spat out, half chewed, onto the floor. "The middle is cold, and the bottom's burnt."

"You were late," I said, reaching for the plate. "I only just started reheating it. Let me fix it for you. The rest will be hotter now."

He swept the plate from my grasp. The rare porcelain hit the wood floor and shattered, sending meat, gravy, and chunks of potatoes and carrots flying.

I jumped to my feet, my heart pounding against my rib cage.

"So it's my fault?" he shouted, spittle flying from his mouth. "My fault? I give you everything. A roof over your stupid head. Food for yer lyin' trap. Clothes for yer skinny little frame. Even porcelain dinnerware." He was on his feet now, his anger making him seem tall.

I heard Hannah's faint cry. *Don't let him hear her.* From the corner of my eye, I could see the steady glow of her life, even through the mostly closed door of the cupboard.

"Maybe you don't deserve anything I give you!" He grabbed the neck of my dress and tugged, but the fabric didn't give. Instead, I was propelled forward, my head connecting with his chest. He shoved me back into the table, and it skidded several feet across the floor. The cups and utensils clattered to the ground. The sliced bread teetered on the edge.

Hannah let out a wail.

I bolted forward, thinking to somehow grab her and get outside, maybe leave her with a neighbor until Simon calmed down, but he was faster. Catching my hair in his fist, he pulled me back and yanked me around. I slid across the floor to slam my head against the solid oak door.

Hannah's cry grew louder.

"Shut up, shut up, shut up!" Simon screamed. His footsteps to the cupboard were heavy and determined.

Hannah cried harder.

Panic fueled me as I launched myself toward Simon. I reached him as he opened the cupboard door. Little Hannah was in her cradle, her face red and her mouth open. I saw two of her, my head still fuzzy from the blow. She took a breath and let out another scream.

"I said shut up," he growled.

I reached for him, but I was too late. His fist came down on Hannah.

The crying stopped.

His hand was ready for another punch, but I lashed out at him. Anything to stop him from hurting Hannah further. Maybe she was just stunned. Maybe I was imagining that the light around her had gone completely out.

"You leave her alone!" I screamed. "Or I'll tell! I'll tell everyone about the monster you are! And they'll believe me. Hannah hasn't been sick a day in her life. They'll know you're a murderer." It wasn't true. So many took ill and died. No one would think twice about Hannah.

"Whore!" Simon hit me on the side of the head. His next punch took me in the stomach with a blow that was all too familiar. Then I was on the floor and he was on top of me, fists pumping. I felt my teeth cave inward. Blood filled my mouth.

"You won't tell anyone nuthin'. Not ever again!" His hands went around my throat, blocking all the air. "I've seen you making eyes at Barker and even the pastor. Maybe you wonder what it'd be like to be with them. Maybe Hannah belongs to one of them. Eh? She certainly ain't mine."

I tried to shake my head, but his grip was too strong. My sight was foggy on the edges, a sure sign that I would soon pass out. I couldn't let that happen. There might be a chance for Hannah. Maybe the darkness I saw from the cupboard came only because of my own injuries.

Except that Simon's own body glow was so bright I could see it with my eyes closed. I could feel his rage, his sense of betrayal. I also saw an image of the farmer who had just come from England and was working the land two homesteads over. He had a twenty-year-old daughter with silky black hair. Simon was already planning my replacement.

My sight darkened. Before I passed out completely, the pressure on my throat eased. I tried to move, but my body refused to obey. Everything hurt. Worse than anything I'd ever known. When I finally pried my eyes open, I saw Simon, his pants around his knees, felt him pushing up my dress. My underclothes ripped. His weight pressed down on me.

His face was close to mine. He was breathing heavy, not with exertion now, but with arousal. "Just one thing left I've been wanting to try," he grated. A knife glinted next to my cheek. "Once, I almost . . . but I didn't. Don't need no potion for this."

He had prepared for this moment. Maybe not exactly like this, but he'd planned my murder. Maybe because he'd decided he didn't want me anymore, or because that new farmer's daughter might give him sons. He slid the knife down, and in a single motion, swiped it across my throat, cutting deeply. I gasped for breath, but none came. The blood welled.

Simon gave a deep laugh that sounded demented. His body trembled against me.

I felt strangely disconnected. I didn't care, not for me. Not with Hannah gone. I couldn't even feel or care about what he was doing.

Maybe I'd finally found my luck like the first Mrs. Brumbaugh.

Except it wasn't the end but only the beginning.

CHAPTER 2

BIRDS CHIRPED HAPPILY IN THE TREES. THE SUN FELT WARM ON my cheek but not on the rest of my face. A cool wind swept through, and the heat on my cheek wavered.

I had to get up. In the next room, Hannah might be awake and need me. I'd have to get Simon's breakfast before he'd finished with the livestock in the barn. That meant hauling the water, building the fire, gathering the eggs.

I stretched, slowly in case it was earlier than I thought and Simon was still in the bed.

Crackling leaves were the first indication that I wasn't where I thought I was. The warmth of the sun and the breeze I'd felt weren't coming from an open window at all.

My eyes flew open. Above me trees loomed, their leaves rustling in the gentle wind. I became aware of sticks and stones digging into my back. My breath came faster, my head rocked back and forth as I looked around, trying to determine where I was.

Nothing was familiar. I was in the middle of the woods, in a place I didn't recognize. Had I been hurt? What was I doing here? How long had I been lying on the ground?

Simon would be angry.

Hannah!

The thought bolted me to a sitting position. My sweet baby! I needed to get back to her. A glance down at myself showed me fully clothed, but the top of my dress was stained with something dark and stiff. Maybe blood. Where it had come from, I couldn't say, because I didn't appear to be hurt. Using a nearby tree, I pulled myself to my feet, feeling dizzy. Which way was home? I had to get back to Hannah.

I stumbled three steps before I saw her. My sweet baby, in her white, multilayered dress that I had worked so hard on during the weeks after her birth. The side of her face was caved in and an insect crawled over her darkened skin.

Memories came rushing back. Simon's fist crashing down on my precious Hannah. The beating, the knife slicing my throat, his weight on my body.

Hannah!

Collapsing to my knees, I began heaving violently. Over and over. Nothing came up. Not even yellow bile.

When the tortured spasms passed, I crawled to my baby and picked her up, cuddling her limp body next to my chest. Stench wafted up to me, bringing to mind a rotting calf I'd once found with its foot caught in a fence. A calf that had been missing for several weeks.

My mouth opened in a silent scream. I stared at the sky, shoulders heaving, clutching my baby.

My baby! My baby! Oh, sweet Hannah!

It was my fault. I should have left the second I found out I was expecting her. But my fear of Simon had frozen me in place. I'd found a journal tucked in a corner, belonging to his first wife. She wrote that he'd threatened to kill her if she ever tried to leave. She'd thought about killing herself.

I'd stayed, thinking that was the only way to save Hannah. To keep her alive until Simon died—he was already past fifty and had lived much longer than most men I'd known.

Yet I knew the truth. I, Ava O'Hare, had been afraid. Afraid of him finding me and the revenge he'd take. Afraid of how we would survive alone. Afraid of everything.

I killed her. It's all my fault.

The silent scream finally found voice, ripping out of my throat and piercing the quiet. My heart broke again and again as I relived the nightmare and my guilt. At last the screams became body-shaking sobs. All that was left was the deathly stillness of the little body in my arms and the pain that filled every portion of my soul.

I didn't know why I was still alive, and apparently unwounded. Had I imagined Simon's anticipation as he choked the breath from me? Had I imagined the hot slicing of the knife? Nothing made sense. Not how I was still alive or why Simon hadn't buried me so no one would discover his depravity.

Yet in the end, none of that really mattered. I didn't care about anything but Hannah.

Time passed. A day. Two. Or maybe three. I didn't know. Twice I slept, still holding Hannah's empty shell, immune to the smell. I wanted to die. Knew that I would eventually without food and water. But I only grew stronger. I felt no hunger, no physical pain. Though I didn't put anything in my mouth, I felt the taste of leaves on my tongue.

The third time I awoke, the agony of Hannah's death had burned to a hard ball in the pit of my stomach. Numbness had taken its place.

Still holding her, I stood and began walking. I didn't know where I was, but I couldn't stay in that place anymore. Trees filled my sight in every direction, giving me no sign of which way to go. In the glimpses of sky between the trees, the sun angled across the peaceful blue expanse, telling me I was heading east. I trudged on. At last I came to a river.

I knew that river. Following it, I eventually came to a section of our property. Simon hadn't shown much creativity in where he'd dumped us, but it was unlikely that our bodies would be found until he started a search. Had anyone even noticed I was missing? Simon had allowed me no friends, and only Mrs. Adamson would question my disappearance when I didn't deliver her embroidery.

If Simon planned to marry the new farmer's daughter, he'd have to report my death, or have someone find my body.

Except that I wasn't dead. I still couldn't figure out why.

The sun told me it was midday, and Simon should be out in the fields. I found a shovel in our barn and began moving again along the river, still heading east, still carrying Hannah. Walking along this river was one of the few freedoms I'd had, and I had wandered far past our property on the rare days when Simon was out of town and my prolonged absence wouldn't be missed.

I stopped at a place some distance from the river, still on our property, where the river widened and a large, gnarled oak tree stood watch as it had for dozens of years. I'd once entertained the thought of tying a rope to its lower branches and fashioning a swing for Hannah.

It was near this tree I buried her now. I dug a deep hole, lining it with a bed of leaves, and wrapped her in my petticoat before placing her inside. "Sleep in peace, my sweet Hannah," I whispered. Sobs once again shook my body as I filled in the hole, though I believed she was at rest.

My fault. My fault.

I could disappear now, take on a new identity. At thirty, I was old, but I was still strong. Any work I could find would be better than my life with Simon.

With Simon, who would now remarry. Another wife, more babies, more deaths.

Those would be my fault too.

That's why he didn't bury me, I thought. *He wanted someone to find us. He'd blame the murders on some fugitive or indigent, and he'd be free to abuse another woman.*

My tears dried. Clutching the shovel, I began walking.

CHAPTER 3

I WAITED UNTIL LATE IN THE AFTERNOON IN CASE SIMON appeared for the noon meal. But apparently, he'd eaten in town. Maybe even visited the brothel. I didn't care. He'd return eventually.

The kitchen looked as if a storm had come through. Dirty, food-caked dishes lay everywhere, the floor had mud tracks and scattered feathers and bones from the chicken Simon had apparently remembered how to kill and cook. There was no fire in the grate or water in the barrel. No fresh bread or butter. He hadn't replaced me yet.

I went to work, first going to the barn where I fed the hungry chickens, catching one to cook for dinner. While I waited for the water to boil so I could begin cleaning off the feathers, I hauled more water to heat for a bath. After spicing the chicken and adding potatoes and vegetables from the bin in the closet, I bathed, washing my long hair and changing into my best Sunday dress that I kept in the cedar chest in Hannah's room.

I needed clean undergarments, and those were in the bedroom I'd shared with Simon, which was as big a mess as the kitchen. There I found what I needed, as well as discarded clothing on the floor that was definitely not mine. My other everyday dress was missing.

The third bedroom looked the same as always, crammed full of farming equipment and Simon's sales manifests. In the top drawer of the old desk, next to several big horse pills, I found the small black bottle of liquid and carried it carefully to the kitchen, setting it on my worktable. I began cleaning the floor as the chicken sizzled in the copper kettle over the fire. The aroma was heady, but I had no real appetite. I thought of the tree and my sweet Hannah. Perhaps I should have dug the grave large enough for me.

The kitchen looked almost normal before I felt him coming. Down the road as usual on Old Bob. Without looking out the window, I picked up a bowl and ladled steaming chicken stew into it, setting it on the table in the place where I normally sat. Then I got another bowl for Simon.

I sat and picked up my spoon. The broth tasted as good as it smelled, probably the best I'd ever made.

The door burst open. Simon stopped and stared as he saw me, his jaw going slack. I smiled, knowing the emotion wouldn't reach my eyes. "Good evening, Simon.

I've made you dinner. It's hot and ready." I stared at him, my gaze not wavering.

He swallowed noisily, the blood seeping from his face. His muddy eyes looked as big as the pit I'd dug for our daughter's grave. He crossed himself and blinked.

"Come on, Simon. Why don't you sit and eat? I'm sorry, I haven't been around, but I'm back now." I stood and motioned for him to take his place.

He backed away, not out the door, but toward the window. "You . . . how . . . I . . ."

I laughed. "What's wrong, Simon? You look like you've seen a ghost. Come on, eat. You'll see your daughter soon. I know how much you love her." I walked over to the door, shutting it.

He still made no move toward the table.

I picked up a knife. "Sit," I ordered.

He scurried to the table and picked up his spoon, his eyes still fixed on me in horror.

I sliced one of the dry biscuits I'd made to go with the stew. There hadn't been time to make bread or butter, but the biscuits would taste good soaked in stew broth. "I'm going to make more pot roast tomorrow," I said, "if we have any meat left from the butchering. You remember the last time we had pot roast, don't you?"

He was gulping down the stew now, though it had to be too hot for such rapid consumption.

I laid the knife down and joined him at the table. "How long has it been?" I pressed. "The last pot roast. The one that was too cold."

He swallowed again noisily. "But you're . . ."

"What?" I smiled. "I'm what, Simon?"

"You're dead." He swallowed the food in his mouth, his spoon clutched tightly in his gnarled hand. "I saw you . . . I . . ."

"You saw what, Simon?" When he didn't reply, I added, "I'm obviously not dead, as you can see. Isn't the stew delicious? I made it just the way you like it."

He nodded, his thick neck bobbing like the chicken I'd beheaded hours earlier. He lowered his eyes, spooning in the broth and chunks of chicken with the same desperation as before. I sipped my own stew, the flavors exploding in my mouth, reminding me that I still had no answer.

"How long would you say I've been gone?" I asked. "You looked so surprised to see me. I can't really remember what happened. It's all a blur." I tilted my head and waited to see if he'd detect the lie. I always could.

With the comment, more color seeped into his face. "T-two weeks," he said.

"What happened?"

He stared at me for several seconds before gulping more stew as if he hadn't eaten during all the time I'd been gone. I didn't interrupt him, but let him spoon it all down and cram in the biscuit without once dipping it into the broth. He tipped the bowl to his mouth and slurped up the rest of the liquid.

"Would you like some more?"

He shook his head. "N-no." This time it was difficult for him to push out the word.

I stood and retrieved the small black bottle, setting it on the table near his bowl. "Last time you made me take two spoonfuls. You've just taken four. You're larger, so I thought it might take more. I hope I didn't give you too much."

He tried to speak, but it came out a jumbled, unintelligible mess. I smiled and finished my stew without saying a word. Then I arose, taking our dishes to the sink. But these I wouldn't be washing. I would never wash dishes again. I picked up the knife from the worktable and brought it back to Simon. I rubbed the side of the blade against his cheek. My mind screamed at me to plunge it into his heart, to cut off his hand or his manhood, but I wouldn't be rushed.

I drew the blade lightly over his throat, just enough to bring a few beads of blood. "Remember this?" I asked. I could see that he did. He remembered it all. And like me, he had no idea how I'd survived. I could feel his emotions as I always had this past year: his fear, his shame, his anger. Even now he wished he could move his limbs so he could kill me again.

And Hannah.

A sob shook me and I turned away, stepping out of his sight so he wouldn't see my pain. The knife clattered to the floor. I felt nearly blinded, agonized, with grief. How could I go on without her, especially knowing it was my fault?

I couldn't, of course, and that was why I was still here.

With the tongs, I pulled out one of the smaller logs from the fireplace, placing it under the table. Then I heaped on the piles of clothes I'd gathered: Simon's work clothes, the rest of mine, and even those left from Simon's prostitute. I didn't look at the monster that was my husband until the table was burning.

"No more," I said to Simon, whose eyes glittered with fear and hatred. "No more dead babies. Or dead wives. No more prostitutes. No more cheating or lies. It's over. You built this house with your own hands, and now you will see it destroyed by the freak you created. By me."

Fire licked at his shoe.

I left the kitchen, going back to Hannah's room. In the cedar chest that had once been my mother's, I swept up the tin box that held my most dear memories. Hannah's first little outfit, barely outgrown, the stuffed bear my mother had made for me as a child that I had planned to share with Hannah. The gold necklace that had belonged to the mother of my first love, Gabriel, a gift from her wealthy parents before she'd run away to marry Gabriel's father. She'd died when Gabriel was only ten, and he'd given me the necklace when I was sixteen, along with a rose that had long since dried and was crumbling. These treasures were all I had left of those I loved.

I slumped to the floor. Hannah's cradle was still in the kitchen cupboard where I'd left it last, but I felt close to her here. *I love you Hannah. I'll be with you soon.*

Something inside, a slice of sanity that remained,

screamed at me to get away. Another part of me cried out that I should have been more humane, even to Simon. I should have at least knocked him unconscious before setting the fire. As it was, he wouldn't be able to cry or scream, but he'd feel himself burning. When he'd given the potion to me, I had felt everything he'd done to my body.

During the afternoon planning, I purposely hadn't thought about any of the good times we had shared together, but they came now: a dance we had attended two months after our marriage, the time our crops had sold for twice what we'd expected, the day he had brought home the porcelain dinnerware.

I was doomed. Maybe by taking revenge, I'd made a pact with the devil himself.

I sensed Simon then. I felt the flames as they spread up his clothes in a deceptively gentle rush before sinking in and biting deep. I experienced his suffering, his regret—not regret that he'd hurt me, but regret that he hadn't done a better job of killing me.

I was burning—consumed by fire. No, *he* was burning. The flames hadn't yet reached the nursery, but in my misery, I'd forgotten we were connected, that I would feel his terror and anguish as if they were my own.

Greedy fire. Horrific agony. So much torture I didn't think I'd live long enough to feel actual flames on my own skin. I brought my hands to my head, clamping down, pushing him away.

All at once the agony stopped and I was aware of my

surroundings again, though I knew he wasn't yet dead. I still had an awareness of the glow that signaled his life, but I'd somehow separated myself from his pain.

I clung to my tin more tightly. Shattering glass echoed throughout the house. The glass Simon had been so proud of when he'd had it put in before any of the neighbors.

Smoke curled into the room, quickly becoming huge billows of gray. I began coughing. I could already feel the heat from the fire. For the first time since laying my baby in her grave, I was scared. Scared to feel the flames again. The agony.

Shame filled me. I couldn't even die right.

Clutching the tin, I scrambled to my feet and ran for the window.

CHAPTER 4

I FELL OUTSIDE, CUTTING MYSELF ON THE BROKEN GLASS. THEN I rolled away, my lungs gasping for breath. I made it as far as the dirt road in front of the house, and there I stood numbly, watching the house burn . . . and burn . . . and burn. Smoke gathered in a cloud, visible in the summer evening.

I was a coward. I'd been able to avenge my daughter's death, and the babies before her, but I hadn't been able to join her. Even now, I trembled as I thought about the flames eating my flesh.

A movement from the edge of my vision startled me. At first I thought it was Simon, somehow freed from the potion's spell and rising like a phoenix from the fire, but two faces came into sight from around the side of the house, a man and a woman.

The man saw me and began to run in my direction.

I cringed away from him as he reached out, but he let his arm drop without touching me.

"Are you all right?" he asked in an accent that sounded both lyrical and familiar.

My eyes flew up to meet those of the most handsome man I'd ever seen. His face was cleanly shaven, his blond hair slightly long but neat, and his well-built figure was set off by stylish clothing like the kind I'd only seen from afar at Mrs. Adamson's. He looked upset, but I knew his anger wasn't directed at me.

"Are you all right?" he repeated.

I shook my head, unable to speak. He reached for me again, but I stumbled away from him.

"Stop. You're scaring her." The woman was somehow on my other side, though I hadn't seen her move, and she was breathtakingly beautiful. Her thick mass of brown hair was artfully pinned on top of her head, her face was delicate but not at all pale, her dark eyelashes were the longest I'd ever seen. Uncaring of her own fine apparel, she enfolded me with her arms. "You're Ava, aren't you?" When I nodded, she continued, her accent matching that of the man. "Good. Then we have come in time."

It's proper English, I thought. Not like the language spoken by the new farmer and his family, but the educated kind.

"Come. It's not safe here," the woman continued. "We're too close to the house. It'll all burn before the neighbors get enough water to help."

That's right. The neighbors would see the smoke.

Simon was disagreeable enough that they wouldn't be quick to check on his property, but they would eventually come. I felt more than a little satisfaction knowing they would be too late to save Simon.

"Hurry now," the woman urged, propelling me several feet. She was strong for her slight stature.

I found my voice. "You don't understand. I killed him. *I* started the fire." When they didn't react, I added, "On purpose."

It felt good to let it out. Let them deliver me to the lawmen. I would take my punishment, welcome it even. Especially if it stopped this horrible longing for Hannah. The numbness had faded, and I didn't want to feel any more pain.

The man gazed at me, compassion radiating from his very blue eyes. "He was an awful man. We both know that."

Something clicked inside me. *He knows!* Somehow the man knew what Simon had been.

"He killed my baby," the words came tumbling from my mouth and more: the lost babies, the numerous times he'd forced himself on me, waking in the woods, burying Hannah, the potion. "I don't care what they do to me. I deserve it. Just when it's over, can you bury me with my baby?"

Tears came to the woman's eyes. "I'm sorry we were so late," she said, her voice like soothing music. "So sorry. We had no idea of course. We've not seen you since you were a child." The woman looked hardly older than I did, so I found that difficult to believe, but I was in too much pain to really care.

"I'm going to see my baby now," I said, glancing beyond the fire in the direction of the tree and the grave.

"Now is not the time," the woman insisted. To the man, she added, "There will be questions if we don't get her out of here before they come." She motioned toward the horizon where already we could see dust above the road that signaled our neighbors' approach.

I glanced between the strangers. Something was odd here. Even the glow surrounding them was dimmer than with most people, closer to the aura of the animals. And I couldn't feel the customary jumble of emotions that emanated from most people. It was as if they were . . . *blocking.* The thought startled me. *Why would I think that?* They were sympathetic, I felt that much—or maybe I only saw it in their faces.

The man's hand touched my shoulder. "Please, come with us. We have been looking for you these past weeks. We want to help."

For a startling moment, I could see into his soul. Feel him as if he were a part of me. It went far deeper than the emotions I'd experienced even from Simon. Not only did the man want to help, he wanted me. Not as a man wanted a woman, but as a father wanted his child. "Who are you?" I whispered.

"I'm Wymon Tilmock, and this is my wife, Eva. We're . . . you might say we're distant relatives on your mother's side. In fact, your name, Ava, is a variation of Eva's."

Eva smiled, looking more beautiful than ever. "Please, will you come with us? We'll explain everything. You need to trust us."

I nodded and let them lead me to a wagon I hadn't noticed before. Halfway there, my legs gave out and Wymon picked me up, cradling me like an infant. My mind felt wild with grief, but somehow, this close to him, I could more easily bear the burden because I felt as if he shared my grief. He laid me in the back of their wagon and pulled a blanket over me despite the warmth of the evening.

The woman sat beside me instead of up with her husband. As she gave me a drink of water, I knew without her saying anything that she planned to hide me with the blanket when we passed our neighbors. I was too tired to protest.

They were wrong about the neighbors coming to help so soon—I'd been wrong. The cloud was nothing more than Cuthbert Mander and his lawless gang, coming to clean up on our misfortune. Eva pulled the blanket over my face just as I glimpsed the five men atop their horses, spreading out to surround the wagon.

We rolled to a stop, and I knew five muskets were pointed in our direction.

"What we got here? Cuthbert asked. His voice was close, so he must have dismounted. The blanket was ripped off me, and I stared up into Cuthbert's lean face, his long dark hair hanging in lank cords to his shoulders.

"She's been hurt," Eva said, lifting my arm where I'd

been cut going out the window. The bleeding had already ceased, but red smeared the length of my arm.

Cuthbert's eyes fixed on me as they always did when I'd had the misfortune of seeing him at public gatherings. I couldn't help thinking of the suspicious deaths that littered his trail.

"Get out," Cuthbert ordered.

"Please," Eva said. "We need to get her to a doctor."

"Sorry," Cuthbert said with a smile that clearly said he wasn't sorry at all. "We can't let you go warning people about the fire. Not until we're done taking what we want. We need traveling funds."

"You are welcome to anything you find," Wymon said. "We won't stop you."

Cuthbert snorted. "Yeah, I'll make sure of that." He motioned and one of his men tossed him some rope. I clutched the tin from my cedar chest, surprised that it was somehow still in my hands.

Wymon pulled a satchel of coins from inside his vest. "Here's more than you'll ever need. Just let us go."

Cuthbert snatched the purse from his hand. "Don't mind if I do. Just fer that, I might let you ride away. In fact, you and your woman can go right now. But not"—he raised his musket, pointing at Wymon's chest—"with our Mrs. High-and-Mighty Brumbaugh." He held my gaze so I would know exactly what he meant. "You think I ain't good enough, don't you? Got so you won't even say good day to a gentleman."

My ignoring Cuthbert had been because of Simon's

jealousy, of course, so maybe Simon would get his revenge on me from the grave.

"Get her out, boys," Cuthbert ordered "I'm going to have me a little fun." Rough hands seized my arms, pulling me from the wagon. Eva shifted to a crouch, but she didn't try to stop them. I hadn't expected to live long, but facing Cuthbert like this was too much. Better to die by a bullet. My muscles bunched in preparation.

The second my feet hit the ground, I lunged toward Cuthbert, but the hands of his goons held me tight.

Cuthbert grinned at my desperation. "Let's get her into the trees in case those God-fearing neighbors decide they need to overlook Simon's uncharitable nature and do their Christian duty." To Wymon, he added. "You got thirty seconds to make yerself scarce or I start shootin'."

"Aw, you really lettin' her go too?" one of Cuthbert's rotten-toothed accomplices thumbed at Eva. "She's a pretty one."

"Shut yer trap," Cuthbert retorted.

Panic filled me. Wymon and Eva had no choice but to leave, if they wanted to live. They couldn't risk their lives. Distant relatives or no, they didn't even know me.

The next instant everything changed. Moving so fast my eyes could barely follow, Eva leapt from the wagon, kicking two of our assailants and somehow flattening both men. Before I could take a breath, she landed on her feet and tore into a third man, whipping around to pound him in the face. Wymon was moving as well, obviously skilled though not nearly as fast as Eva. He knocked Cuthbert's musket from his hand, and they began exchanging blows.

"Look out!" I shouted as the fifth member of the gang brought his rifle around to aim at Wymon. I jumped, grabbing at the gun. But Eva and Wymon were already next to me, knocking the man unconscious before he could pull the trigger.

Eva looked at Wymon. "You'll have to take their memories. It's better that her neighbors don't know she's still alive. Hurry—we are about to have more company." She glanced out over the road where another dust cloud hovered.

Wymon knelt down between two of the men, reaching out to touch both their faces. In seconds, he finished with the men and moved on to the third and fourth.

I stared at Eva in fascinated horror. "Who are you? *What* are you?" I'd never seen a woman move like that before, much less one who looked like Eva. And a man who believed he could remove memories with a simple touch? It was unbelievable, though a part of me wished he could take away the past year of my life.

Except that would erase Hannah, and I couldn't let myself forget her. Not ever.

Eva smiled, apparently unruffled by the fight or by her husband's supposed ability. "I'm your tenth great-grandmother. I'm Unbounded—Renegade Unbounded, to be exact. And since you are not dead, apparently, so are you."

PART TWO

Fifty Years Later

September 1795 - Savannah, Georgia

Lemonade and Love

CHAPTER 5

I SMILED DOWN AT THE FRESH LEMONADE MARTHA HAD brought on a silver tray. My fingers closed around the tall, cool glass, and I raised it, saluting Locke MacAulay, the blond-haired woman opposite me. "To your parents."

Locke smiled. "Yes, to my parents."

I sipped the sweet liquid. After my rescue fifty years ago, Eva and Wymon Tilmock had brought me here to Savannah, Georgia, where they had trained me and taught me the ways of the Unbounded, or the Unboundaried, if you wanted to be more correct. Humans whose active Unbounded gene caused them to Change and become part of a rare breed, usually between the thirtieth and thirty-first birthdays. Old injuries healed, barren women gave birth, a husband's knife had no permanent power.

Well, provided a future Unbounded lived long enough to Change.

Wymon had shared my ability of sensing and had

become closer than my own father, but Eva's combat training had given me the confidence I'd desperately needed. Never again would I be a helpless victim—to anyone.

Both Wymon and Eva were gone now, their lives cut short in an ongoing battle with our enemy the Emporium just two years after the close of the Revolutionary War. Their sacrifice had prevented renewed confrontations with England, but I still desperately missed them. I had lost myself in those first years after Hannah's death. They had brought me back from despair and taught me to live again, taught me to understand and accept the Change that made me nearly immortal with a lifespan of two thousand years.

Now I worked with Locke, their daughter and a fellow Renegade, who was my ninth great-grandmother but more like a sister than anything else. Our current goal was to free America from the curse of slavery, even as the slave trade ramped up with the demand brought on by the invention of the cotton gin. We would succeed, but it would take time because the Emporium Unbounded had their own agenda, and the mortals' greed had blinded them to the evils of slavery.

Locke's eyes lifted across the green expanse of grass where we sat at a table in the shade of a tree. It was late afternoon in September and not nearly as hot as it had been a few weeks earlier. "Looks like you have more petitioners," she said, her voice sounding more Scottish like her late mortal husband than her English parents.

AVA'S REVENGE

I turned to see Samuel, our butler, his ever-calm face standing out darkly against his white suit, gliding across the expanse of lawn with a man in tow. The man walked steadily at the butler's side, without hunching his shoulders or averting his eyes as many petitioners did. Something about the way he walked was familiar.

A slight movement in the trees to my left registered on my senses. I knew it was Ritter Langton, who had been brought to us two decades ago, shortly after his Change, by Tenika Vasco, the second-in-command of our Renegades in New York. Tenika had been afraid Ritter's single-minded recklessness would get him killed in their frequent encounters with the Emporium. She'd hoped Eva and Locke could train him, and that somehow along the way Wymon and I could temper the anger he harbored at the brutal murders of his mortal family. In the decade since Wymon's death, I didn't feel I'd made much progress.

Ritter's movement had been purposeful, to let me know he was there watching, just in case. I couldn't feel his anger from this distance, but it was still there. I knew because anger had consumed me in much the same way. It made him both vicious and reckless. I was glad he was on our side.

As I refocused on the approaching stranger, shock flooded me. When Samuel reached the table, he bowed, "A mister Gabriel Smithson to see you, Miss O'Hare."

I nodded, scarcely seeing Samuel's face. I couldn't take my eyes off the newcomer, who was hardly more than a boy of perhaps twenty. Sixty-three years melted away as if they had never been. I was seventeen and he was sixteen, holding my hand as we cried together after my father announced my upcoming marriage to Simon.

No, it couldn't be the boy who had loved me, though he looked exactly like him. I'd turned eighty-one this year, though I had physically aged only one year in the past fifty, and my Gabriel would be eighty. He was probably long dead.

The young Gabriel's eyes went to Locke's deeply plunging neckline where the swell of her breasts stood out against the single roll of blond hair over her left shoulder. He looked away, his face reddening. "Please, Miss," he said to me, "I come to ask the favor of a loan. I will pay it back. I am a hard worker. I'll make my farm a success."

"The blight hit your farm?" This close, I could now detect differences from my Gabriel. The brown eyes were slightly darker, and the blond hair lighter and a bit wavy.

He hesitated at my words, and I opened my mind, reaching out to his. Many had come to me for help in the past years, and most of them had been sincere in their claims. A few had thought to deceive me, to use my kindness to their advantage. I wouldn't delve into all his thoughts, but this way most of his emotions were readily apparent. I would know if he lied.

"No," he said finally. "My father gambled our savings away and took out a loan against the farm. But he's gone now and my grandfather will be leaving the farm to me. If I can keep it from the bank."

His sincerity was clear, but I focused on the brief glimpse I saw of his grandfather in his thoughts. "Who is your grandfather? Where is he from?" Ten years after my Change, I'd checked up on Gabriel from a distance, wanting to know what had happened to him. Perhaps wondering if there was room for him in my life. I'd found him still in Virginia, married with four strapping sons. I was glad he'd had a life, that he'd found a way to go on, even if I couldn't seem to. I'd already known in my heart that there couldn't be any future for us because I was no longer the girl who would be happy as a farmer's wife, and he would never be anything but a farmer.

Gabriel smiled and love emanated from him. "From Williamsburg, Virginia originally. He and my dad and my uncles came here before I was born. But he's all I have left now, and I guess I'm all he has. I'm his namesake, and I'm proud to bear it."

"I have family from Williamsburg. Who were his parents?" A few more questions and I knew without a doubt that fate had once again crossed my life with the boy of my youth. "Is he well?" I asked finally. There was a catch in my voice that made Locke gaze at me more intensely.

Gabriel didn't seem to notice my emotion, his eyes now studying the ice in my lemonade. He must think it a huge waste of money, a curious luxury, but he couldn't know that Unbounded had advanced technology that made ice a simple matter. "Not so much these days," he said, meeting my gaze once more. "He's mostly bedridden and he doesn't see well at all, though his mind is still strong. But I plan to marry soon, and I pray that will ease his burdens." His smiled faded. "That is, if I can . . . I . . ."

I knew what that meant. He wanted to be able to support a wife before plunging into matrimony. From where I sat now, he seemed too young to marry, but mortal lives were short, so they only did what they should.

"You *will* be married." I looked at Samuel, who was still standing, enjoying the shade. "Please bring me a purse. And will you have Martha find my tin box? She'll know what I mean."

"Of course," Samuel bowed. I trusted him with all the running of the house, and like our other workers, he was content. It was a fine line we walked, Locke and I, treating our slaves with respect and trying to work within the system to free them, while at the same time making the cotton plantation support itself. Too often we'd had to use the funds Locke's parents had left us to keep the business afloat or to protect our friends.

When Samuel returned with the tin, he had Gabriel sign the customary promise note, while I removed the necklace that had belonged to Gabriel's mother. Without unwrapping it from its handkerchief, I slipped it into the purse of coins Samuel had also brought. "Don't open this until you get back to your grandfather," I said to Gabriel.

"Thank you from the bottom of my heart." Gabriel bowed to me and then to Locke before turning to stride across the lawn. Even in his humble clothes he looked far more confident than when he'd arrived.

"What was *that* about?" Locke asked, arching a brow.

"I knew his grandfather as a girl."

"I see." She knew there was more, but I wasn't ready to share. I didn't know if I would ever love anyone the way I had Gabriel, but I had a lot of years to figure it out.

Two days later, I was in the library when Samuel appeared. "Someone to see you, Miss O'Hare."

"Who is it?" I looked up from the letter I was writing.

"Gabriel Smithson."

"Show him in here, please." What could he want with me so soon? I hoped it wasn't bad news. Perhaps he'd come to tell me his grandfather was dead.

The thought brought me to my feet, so I was standing when young Gabriel entered. His face was drawn, his eyes filled with pain. "What is it?" I asked. My heart thumped loudly in my chest.

"My grandfather is dying. I'm sorry, but . . . he's asking for you. He won't say why. I expect . . . maybe he wants to thank you."

I called for a carriage and went at once. The farmhouse was larger than I expected, and far more masculine. Gabriel's wife had evidently been dead a long time. I was shown to his room, where I found a frail, wizened figure in a large bed, the light—or life force, as I'd learned it was called—around him faded and weak. As I sat in the chair by the bed, he opened his eyes. Warmth shot through me. He *was* my Gabriel. There was no mistaking the eyes, despite the white haze clouding them.

His gaze shifted to his grandson. "Please, give us a moment."

When the boy was gone, Gabriel took my hand. "Ava." The word sounded like a sigh. "I knew it was you the moment I saw the necklace. But how? You haven't changed a bit."

I had Changed—and far more than he'd ever suspect. "Your eyes are old," I said. "You must be seeing a memory."

"I see well enough." A pause and then, "Ava, I never stopped loving you."

There was no sense in pretending. "Nor I, you."

He smiled at that. "Keep watch over my boy, will you?"

"I will."

PART THREE

Fifty Years Later

April 1845 - Natchez, Mississippi

Free at Last

CHAPTER 6

When Betsy signaled from the back hallway near the hotel dining room, her dark face was flushed, her eyes wild. My jaw hardened as I let the newest letter from Gabriel's second great-grandson fall to my lap. Betsy obviously had found something in her investigation of the slave pens.

I nodded once, letting her know that I would meet her in my rooms. Slaves weren't allowed in the dining area of this upscale hotel, though they could help their owners in the privacy of their own rooms. Betsy had been free for a decade and living in the North for the past five years, but in this town, home to the second largest slave market, it was wise to keep up appearances. Drinking a final casual sip of my afternoon tea, I placed the porcelain cup on the delicate saucer, picked up my reticule, and arose.

"Miss!" A motion to my left had me shifting

imperceptibly into a better defensive position. Despite my layers of petticoats and skirts, no one in the dining room could be much danger, but I was always prepared. I touched the handle of a knife, hidden in the folds of my dress.

A man bent and picked up my letter that had fallen to the richly tiled floor, his muscles rippling under his tailcoat. I caught a glimpse of a red silk vest under the coat. "You dropped this." His eyes bore into me as he stood, and for a moment, I didn't breathe.

Ah, it's you, I thought.

I'd noticed him when I'd come into the dining room. I'd even felt regret that I wasn't in Natchez on some pleasure trip that might allow me to meet him. He had light blond hair with a high widow's peak, intelligent blue eyes, a square jaw, and a bold, confident manner. So confident that if my ability hadn't included being able to instantly identify Unbounded, I might have mistaken him for one of my kind.

He'd also noticed me, and the interest I'd sensed from him earlier was stronger now at close proximity. He handed me the letter, and our eyes held. It was difficult to tell his interest from my own, though I refrained from delving into his more private thoughts.

It's been too long. Too long since I'd let myself care for a man. Here I was acting like a young girl simply because a gentleman had been mannerly.

A really fine gentleman.

I blinked the thoughts away and accepted the letter.

"Thank you. I very much appreciate it. It would have been a great loss to me."

His smile was disarming. "I'm glad then. Though I daresay, I'm jealous of the man."

"Oh, really?" I couldn't stop amusement from seeping into my voice. "How do you know it's from a man?"

"The intentness in your gaze." He inclined his head, his grin still wide. "But he is far away, and I am here. I think it might be important to point this out."

That made me laugh. "Maybe so. I'll think on it."

"It would be my great fortune. I will be here a day or two." He gave a full bow that somehow seemed both to mock and to flatter me. "I won't keep you. I saw your girl wave to you. She looked . . . upset."

His concern for a mere slave intrigued me. "Yes, you are correct. Please, excuse me."

He bowed again, and I forced my curiosity about him to the back of my mind as I hurried out of the room and up the front staircase.

Betsy was waiting in my sitting room, terror for her sister and her family etched across her face. "I saw 'em! Looks like they only jest come t' town. Got 'em in the pen, out in the open, not inside. Like there's too many to fit. They be on the block t'morrow, if'n I guess right."

"Then we'll act tonight. Locke and I will get them out. And Ritter, of course. You must stay here. You've risked enough by traveling here on your own."

Betsy nodded. "I cain't see how sumpin' like this can happen. They was free and happy up North. We all was."

"You will be again." I set my reticule on the narrow wall table next to the door. "If you will, please go inform Locke and Ritter that we need to be ready to go before nightfall."

Betsy took two steps toward the door before she halted and turned around, flinging herself into my arms. "There was nowhere else t' go. I knew you'd help Frances. But don't go gettin' yo'self hurt. You's the only white angel I know."

I returned her exuberant hug. Betsy was my own physical age, and she'd grown up on my plantation in Savannah. She didn't seemed to notice that I hadn't aged while we'd lived together or in the five years since I sent her and her sister, a former slave from a neighboring plantation, north with their families.

"Don't you worry. It'll be all right." My drawl hid my real emotion. Inside I was furious. This wasn't the first time my former slaves had contacted me for help, but it was the first time an entire free family had been stolen from the North and brought back to be sold into slavery.

Since my recent return from England with Locke and Ritter, I'd been hearing more and more about such illegal events happening, and there was no way I was going to sit by and watch as my friends' lives were stolen. If I had my way, this particular slaver, Lucias Johansson, was going out of business—permanently.

Just that fast, Betsy curtsied and was gone. I began removing my skirt to prepare for the evening's adventures. I normally loved the gowns of the south, but my combat training had also taught me how impractical they were. I couldn't be encumbered by skirts tonight. The clock on the fireplace mantel told me I had plenty of time for my disguise.

Excitement rippled through me—my Unbounded genes kicking in. I was ready for action. I craved it. Though we'd recently had two skirmishes with the Emporium in New York City when their agents had tried to assassinate several key political leaders, for the most part I had been in the background. All Unbounded were gifted at something, but my sensing ability was a rare talent and none of our Renegade allies were willing to risk me. After determining the guilty parties, I'd been relegated to watching and waiting.

Neither of which I did well, even when necessary. Maybe it was something I'd learn in the next hundred years or so.

My eyes landed on the letter I'd been reading earlier, sticking partially out of my reticule. Miles Smithson, Gabriel's second great-grandson, had grown up to be a good man, and the money I'd spent educating first his father and then him had been well-employed. Miles had become an attorney-at-law in Alabama and hadn't needed my patronage for years, but I still enjoyed exchanging letters with him. Though I couldn't tell him the full extent of my life, he shared my views on nearly every political issue—especially those regarding slavery.

Of course he might not have had much chance to pursue other opinions. I'd been his family's benefactor since Gabriel senior's death, sending all his posterity to college. Because I was their benefactor, they'd had no choice but to listen to my views, and the more educated they became, the more they understood the world at large and the evils slavery represented.

I'd met Miles only once, when he was a young child. Though I'd promised Gabriel to look after his family, I'd satisfied my duty with letters from afar so that my unchanging appearance wouldn't be noted. Every now and then I made an appearance as some relative—a granddaughter or the granddaughter's niece. It was enough to fulfill my promise and to keep them safe from the Emporium, who would use them as collateral against me if they discovered an opportunity. The Emporium would be happy to capture a sensing Unbounded with an extended lifetime of childbearing in front of her.

At that thought, my stomach tensed. I had almost married again a decade ago, but for the fertile Unbounded, marrying always meant bearing children, and I couldn't. Not then. So I had let him go. I hadn't regretted my decision. Mostly. One advantage of living two thousand years was having plenty of time to change your mind.

Maybe I'd look Miles up on our way back to Georgia. He would be twenty-nine now, only a few years younger than I was, and he wouldn't remember my visit so long ago. I'd be interested in meeting a man who wrote an old lady—or someone he thought was an old lady—such witty and intelligent letters. I'd have to pretend to be an even younger relative than the granddaughter's niece he thought me to be, the woman he'd met as a child. Maybe a cousin this time. I'd have to research what I'd told him.

Humming under my breath, I turned into my bedroom to finish dressing.

Locke's smile grew wide as she took in my appearance. "You make a mighty pretty boy." She was also dressed as a man, and her blond hair was hidden under a hat like mine, but her disguise made her look in need of a good shave instead of a woman wearing a man's clothes. Nothing short of a miracle where the very female Locke was concerned.

Dragging my gaze from the mirror over the bureau, I scowled. "That noticeable, huh?"

Beside her, Ritter barked a laugh. "Your skin. It's not right. Not even close." He peered closer, a sardonic grin on his face. "Is that face powder mixed with coffee grounds?"

I groaned, though a part of me noted the laugh. Even after seventy years of working together, the laughs didn't come frequently enough. His anger still consumed him, but he was more careful now. Maybe in another fifty years he might understand that anger never brought our loved ones back. It only made us different from the people they had loved in life. Maybe we even risked becoming someone they wouldn't care to know.

"I was trying a new process," I said, "but I hadn't tested it yet." I usually did our operations in my dresses—accidentally touching people or pushing my way into their minds to study the sand stream of their thoughts. More often than not, my job was primarily to inform those gifted with other abilities which Emporium agents were Unbounded and which were mortal employees. Only when I was really lucky did I get to use my combat training. This only made me train all the harder because I didn't want to let anyone down if I did have to fight.

Locke opened her bag and began setting out containers on the bureau. "Well, the smell certainly screams *eau de l'homme.*" She meant aroma of man, but the French words lost something in the translation.

Ritter folded his arms across the very wide expanse of his muscled chest. He looked dark, dangerous, and deadly. I sensed he wasn't offended by Locke's comment, his thoughts already far away. A flash of memory filled me: a dark-haired woman in a blue dress, her body severed in three. Ritter's former fiancée, who had been murdered with his family. Severing the body's three focal points—the brain, the heart, the reproductive organs—was one of only two ways Unbounded could be killed. That his fiancée wasn't likely to undergo the Change hadn't mattered to the Emporium. They had been gunning for Ritter, who, after reaching his thirtieth birthday, had Changed, and for his little sister, who had the possibility of Changing one day.

I wished I could convince Ritter that it wasn't his fault, but in the end I didn't think it would matter. His family and the woman he loved were still dead, along with Ritter's Unbounded ancestor who'd arrived barely in time to save him. It was a guilt he'd have to come to terms with or the two thousand years of his life would be long and lonely.

That loneliness I sometimes still felt in my own heart, and on those days, Locke and Ritter and my work weren't enough. I still longed for my Hannah, but I no longer blamed myself for her death, even though ultimately, through my youth and inexperience, I was responsible for it.

"So what's the plan tonight?" Locke asked, as she began fixing my face. She was older than me by more than four centuries but was content to let me lead. She just wanted to fight. Between her and Ritter, who shared her combat ability, I'd have to make sure they didn't have too much fun. Mortals broke easily, and while we wanted to stop the abuse of our friends, our ultimate goal was to protect mortals from the Emporium—and from themselves.

"We'll free Frances and her family from the holding pen," I said. "Then we'll track down Johansson and have a chat with him."

"So we aren't just going to wait until tomorrow to buy Frances's family? It might be better." We'd done it before, but the anticipation in Locke's voice belied her comment. She wanted to put an end to the slaver as much as I did.

"No," I said. "We're going to shut Johansson down."

CHAPTER 7

The cluster of buildings at the Forks of the Road was little more than a dirty prison camp. The sprawling market would sell up to five hundred slaves a day, most bought in Virginia and sold here in the Deep South to cotton plantation owners. Importing slaves from outside the US hadn't been legal for over forty years, but the domestic breeding and slave trade abounded. The profit was huge and even larger when the slaves weren't really slaves at all like Betsy's family.

Anger burned in me. We'd helped thousands of former slaves over the years, and our Renegade allies were active in politics, fighting to end slavery altogether, but the greed of humanity—and the Emporium, who had fingers in every large slaving company—meant that it would likely be years before the end came altogether.

One life at a time, I told myself.

Most of the slavers had marched their so-called property to Natchez like cattle, boating them only part of the way. Here they would be bathed, clothed, and then haggled over like a mule or a wagon. The indignity aside, being torn from their homes and loved ones was something they never got over.

I knew because I felt their emotions, and they were every bit as human—perhaps more so—as those who treated them like animals.

Rough wooden buildings partially circled the slave holding pen, the spaces between the buildings enclosed with wood fencing, tin scraps, or whatever was at hand. A large gate led into a courtyard. Inside the buildings, slave men and women and children were kept at night and bargained over during the day. But Betsy had seen Frances and her family in the courtyard with others, constructing makeshift tents or simply collapsing on the ground. That told me the market was unusually full, but the coming summer did mean higher profits, so it wasn't surprising.

We investigated the entire area from the outside and formulated a plan, noting the positions of the few patrolling guards. In the fading evening light many of the exhausted slaves in the courtyard resembled sacks of flour lumped on the ground. Evening came early in April and could be deathly cold, though tonight it was still relatively mild. I hoped the good weather would hold.

A child's cry cut through the night. A child who by morning might never see his mother again.

"Wait for the signal," I told the others. I was going inside to find Frances.

Locke and Ritter nodded, fanning out along the perimeter. I didn't have to tell them to watch for the patrol. Locke and Ritter both knew their job, and I'd signal with the pistol I carried in my holster under my coat if things got out of control.

Getting inside shouldn't be a problem. I carried a crate of white cotton shirts that matched those the slavers distributed, and while I was older than most delivery boys, I knew how to get through. I approached the two guards at the gate entrance, my eyes down on the ground.

"What you got there?" With the squeak of a leather boot, one of the guards stepped in front of me. He reeked more of *eau de l'homme* than I'd smelled on any man since Simon had grunted over my body after a full day of work in the fields. His long brown hair looked greasy enough to oil my gun.

"More shirts. They need 'em before morning. Gotta get them Negroes up to snuff."

"Who they for?" asked his partner. His hair fell into his mean eyes, and a vertical scar ran down the center of his cheek from his eye to his jaw, looking awfully similar to the fake one Locke had fashioned across my cheek. I hoped he didn't expect me to trade war stories.

"Oh, it's that tall dude. Should be in the courtyard. Mister, uh . . ." I was gambling a little, but there seemed to be too many slaves in the courtyard to belong only to Johansson, and for now I didn't want to be remembered in connection with him since I planned to steal Frances and her family away from here. Reaching out, I used my proximity to push into the long-haired guard's mind. There his thoughts ran in a stream that resembled sand angling from the top right of my vision and vanishing near my lower left, each grain representing a thought, and not always a conscious one. I saw almost immediately what I needed. "Mister Armstead," I said.

"He ain't that tall." This from the first man, who was rather short.

I shrugged, not meeting his eyes. "Everybody's tall to me."

He barked a laugh and puffed out his chest. "That's true enough."

"You'll find Armstead's Negroes that way." The mean-eyed fellow threw out an arm in the opposite direction I wanted to go. Oh well.

I took a step forward. "Thank you."

"Wait." Hard fingers gripped my shoulder. Mean-eyes, of course. "Don't you got somethin' for us? You know the rules. It's after hours."

I pulled a bottle of gin from under the shirts. "Right. Almost forgot." They took the bottle, laughing greedily, and didn't stop me from hurrying away.

Before long I was weaving around the clumps of people, many dead to the world after their gruesome march, their dark skin blending into the night. Every so often a sob reached my ears, but for the most part an eery silence reined. A silence of despair and hopelessness.

I ducked around a tent that tonight was being used as a bathhouse. Several guards were peeping in, watching a group of slave women through large gaps in the cloth. Some women used their bodies as shields for others as they bathed. I burned with anger. I could take out all the guards but not before they raised an alarm. I angled away from the tent.

Somewhere a deep mournful voice was singing, words in a language passed down by their fathers. I'd learned several dialects, but this one wasn't familiar, and I understood only a few words. The notes caught at me, begging for freedom, for escape. I pushed on.

I found Frances and her family in a group beyond one of the smaller buildings. She sat holding her daughter, Mabel, a child of ten, who was wrapped in a thin blanket. Tears marked Frances's face as she rocked back and forth soundlessly.

Her husband, James, lay on a tarp, his arms spread protectively over their two teenage boys' huddled forms, giving the children what warmth he could. James was gaunt and looked miserable. He had to be exhausted, but his eyes were open and searching the sky. Searching for what?

I didn't know.

I approached slowly. Fear blossomed in Frances's eyes as she spotted me. "Don't worry," I said, in my own voice. "I have something for you."

"They give us clothes already," she said.

James sat up, abruptly becoming aware of my presence.

His fists clenched. He was wearing the white shirt, plain pants, and sturdy shoes of a slave about to be sold.

I glanced around, fearing that some of the other slaves nearby would hear. There was little hope of privacy. I had to get closer. James moved as I did, clearly ready to protect his wife.

I went to my knees at her side. "It's me, Ava O'Hare."

Frances's eyes widened, and she motioned for James to squat down with us. "Thank de blessed Lawd," Frances said. "I knew ya'd come."

I didn't tell her that we almost hadn't made it in time. If Betsy hadn't sold everything she owned and sent a rider to me with a message to meet her here, if she hadn't been able to find out that the slaver Johansson was heading to Natchez, and if we hadn't ridden hard to beat them here, everything would have worked out differently. My anger burned again. Too many ifs.

"My baby," Frances said. "She burnin' with fever. James carried her most all de way from de North. I cain't lose her."

"You won't. But we have to move closer to that building back there. Next to it there's a length of wood fence. James, wake the boys and tell them to go there. But have them circle around. We can't risk drawing attention." I flicked my eyes in the right direction. "Go slow. Don't call attention to yourself. You know how the guards are." They wouldn't shoot unless they had to, because they considered the Negroes valuable livestock, but killing one that was trying to escape would bring about less guilt than putting down an old horse.

"Yes, Miss." James's eyes met mine, hope replacing his former desolation. "Thank ye fer comin'."

"Hurry," I said. Some of the sleepers around us were waking now, and though we'd been quiet, their eyes were watchful.

I arose and said louder to Frances in my practiced male voice, "Come with me. I have medicine to dose the child. Mister Johansson won't be happy if he can't get a sale tomorrow. If you're lucky, you'll go together. But only if she's better."

A sob caught in Frances's throat at the words that we both knew were truth—or would have been if I hadn't come. But we'd gone only a few paces when Frances whispered. "What 'bout de others?"

"Others?"

"More'n sixty-five of us, I think."

I stepped closer to her, accidentally bumping her in my shock. "Sixty-five? Taken from the North?"

"'Bout forty from de North. We was met partway by others come from Virginia. And dat man what brought de others—" She gave me a frightened look, her eyes glistening in the darkness. "I never saw de like. I think he de real boss man. Put me in mind of Massa Ritter. But meaner."

Ritter would correct her if he'd heard Frances use that title. He wasn't anyone's master, he'd say, but some habits were hard to break, and Frances wasn't about to change now. Her description bothered me, because Unbounded were different from other people, but to people without my gift, it came across as striking beauty and confidence. In a rich drawing room where everyone looked their best, it wasn't as noticeable, but in a setting like this, where so many men were missing teeth, had scars, or were withered by the sun, Unbounded always stood out.

"De others," Frances said into the silence. "They has chillens."

More children. My mind raced. *One thing at a time. Think about the others after you free Frances.*

"You!" a shout came from across the courtyard.

Frances stiffened. "Let me do the talking," I said. Not that she'd speak anyway; she looked too frightened. Even if I had to fight my way out, I trusted that Ritter and Locke would be ready to back me up.

A man came striding across the sea of captives, those who were awake cringing away from him and his two companions. His life force glowed dimmer than everyone else's in the area, signaling a blocked mind.

That wasn't all my ability confirmed. Mortals could also block, those who learned how, but this man was definitely Unbounded, and that meant the Emporium was here.

CHAPTER 8

I WOULD HAVE GUESSED THAT HE WAS UNBOUNDED EVEN without my ability by the way he carried himself. As if he owned not only the Forks of the Road but all of Mississippi. Emporium Unbounded saw themselves as gods, and all mortals as little more than slaves to be used and discarded as desired. If they had their way, this place would someday see white flesh mixed in with the black. Even if combat wasn't his ability, this Unbounded was likely trained, and the double pistols at his sides certainly weren't for looks.

Yet as long as he didn't share my ability and couldn't tell that I was Unbounded, I still had an advantage. The two mortals accompanying him had bright life forces, but they carried rifles, useless in close fighting. They would not be a concern unless I let down my guard. I reached into my crate and began moving objects.

"What's going on here?" the Unbounded demanded.

I briefly met his stare before looking down like any subservient would. He wasn't an Unbounded I'd ever met or one we had listed in our files. He also hadn't seemed to mark me as Unbounded, so he didn't share my particular ability. "I am employed by the city of Natchez. As you know, we can't risk an outbreak of disease, which is why we have the Forks set up away from town. I am examining this child. She might be contagious."

"You're a doctor?"

"Only an assistant." I let a little derision slip into my voice, telling everyone within range know that I considered treating "livestock" beneath even an assistant.

He gazed down into the crate I carried, but instead of the white shirts, the top items were now bottles of chemicals and powders. "You do not have permission to remove them from the courtyard." Arrogance dripped from the words.

"That won't be necessary. Are you Lucias Johansson?"

"Nah. He's John Cardiff," said one of the henchmen. "Johansson works for him. These Negroes are his property."

When Cardiff didn't refute him, I said, "I need space to check this child." I pointed to a place some ten feet away from a length of wood fencing. Not where Ritter and Locke waited, but it would have to do.

Cardiff's gaze fell on Mabel, and I took the opportunity to study him. Dark eyes framed by thick black lashes. A head of dark hair that was slightly wavy and looked freshly washed. A narrow, recently shaven, face that would have been compellingly attractive except for the cruel set of his jaw. Clean clothes that fit his figure well and not so much hinted at but screamed wealth.

I wanted to stab my knife into his heart.

He pointed a finger at Frances. "Put the child down over there and get back with the others. The *assistant* here will bring back the whelp if it survives."

Ignoring Frances's swift intake of breath, Cardiff jerked his hand, and one of his goons jabbed his rifle into her, keeping well away from Mabel. Frances stumbled forward. At the place I'd indicated, she laid Mabel down, tucking the thin blanket around her small figure.

Frances stared at me, her eyes pleading. "Please, Massa, keep my babe safe." I knew what she was saying, for me to save Mabel and the rest of her family, even if I couldn't come back for her.

"Git!" said the man with the rifle at her back. "I see you back here, and I'll put a bullet through yer head!"

Frances fled. Without another word, the Unbounded and his companions turned and stalked away.

Now what? I felt Mabel's forehead. She moaned and her eyes opened with a fluttering.

"Shush now," I said. "It'll be okay."

"Who are you?" Her brow furrowed in concentration.

"I'm a friend of your Aunt Betsy."

"They took my book," she murmured, tears filling her voice. "Said Niggurs like me can't read. It was my only book."

"I'll get you another one. I promise."

I sent my mind out, reaching for Ritter and Locke. I hoped they were close enough. There. A life force near the fence. Ritter. And he was even more angry than usual. I felt the emotion, though not the reason.

Making sure no one watched me, I whistled. Seconds later, Ritter knelt by the fence.

"What about the guards?" I asked.

"They won't bother us. Where's Frances?"

"I'll have to go back for her."

"Scoot the child closer."

I heard a sawing noise as he worked at the bottom pole. I held up a bottle, pretending to examine its contents, but in reality, I was searching for watching eyes. "There's a man over there paying us a little too much attention," I whispered. "You're in enough shadow that he won't be able to see you, but he'll certainly notice if I push her through the fence."

The sawing stopped briefly. "You'd better have a talk with him."

I bent closer to Mabel and whispered. "This nice gentleman is a friend. He's going to take you to your daddy. Don't make any noise. Understand?"

She nodded, the fear in her eyes tying a knot in my throat.

"If you can't get Frances out at the original location," Ritter said, "meet me at the rendezvous. We'll formulate another plan."

Giving Mabel a comforting pat, I stood and walked

toward the slave who'd kept glancing in our direction, the only man awake in a group of huddled people. He was a big man with a prominent forehead and arms that went on forever. But like James, he was gaunt and appeared exhausted.

"You sick?" I asked. "I work for the city. We can't have sickness spreading to the town."

"No, Massa, I ain't sick." His voice was higher than I expected and docile.

I saw a rag sticking out of his pants and the slight darkness of a stain below the knee. "Roll up your pants."

He blinked. "Ain't nothin' wrong."

"I'll help you. Please."

He blinked in surprise at my words. Still, with great reluctance the big man rolled up his pant leg. The rag he'd tied around his calf was soaked with blood.

"I'm going to have to look at it."

The knots were too tight to untie, and he made no objection when I took scissors from my crate and cut it off. A gaping wound met my efforts. "This needs stitching." I looked around and grabbed a stick from the dirt, handing it to him. "Bite down on this. Sorry, but it's going to hurt." I'd seen men take fever and die from lesser wounds.

I splashed alcohol around the wound and began stitching. I wasn't a healer, but every Renegade learned to patch people up. To the man's credit, he didn't utter a peep, though rivulets of sweat rolled down his face. When I had finished with fifteen neat stitches, I used clean bandages to wrap it, then I handed him a pill from one of the bottles. "Take this. It'll make sure you don't get a fever."

He swallowed it without question. The drug was one that our Renegade healers had invented for mortal use, though we estimated that it would be another hundred years before mortal technology began to catch up. We'd helped fund studies involving mold, but there was only so much we could do without making our existence known. The slow-release antibiotic would stay in the man's system for a week—hopefully long enough. If the night weather didn't turn warmer soon, or if he wasn't given a blanket, he still might not survive.

I glanced back to where I'd left Mabel, but she was gone. "Musta gone back to her momma," the big man said, seeing my gaze.

"Guess she's feeling better. Look, in this many days"—I held up two hands and then one more—"these threads have to come out. The swelling will have gone down. All you do is cut off the knot and pull it out. One of the women should be able to do it for you."

He nodded. "Fifteen days."

I had underestimated him. Over the years I'd made sure the slaves on my plantation could count and read, and I'd given secret lessons to their families who lived nearby, but many slave owners felt doing so was dangerous to their superiority. "That's right. Fifteen days."

It took a few more moments to extract myself from his exuberant thanks, but the more time that passed without alarms being raised, the more likelihood that Ritter and Locke had managed to get James and the children free. Now if I could do the same for Frances, we'd be in the clear.

I didn't fool myself that Johansson wouldn't eventually notice five missing "slaves," and Cardiff was even less likely to let it slide. But my plans for disrupting Johansson's entire operation had to wait now that there was an Emporium agent in charge. We'd need more Renegade agents and deeper intel on their operation before we moved on them, because in all probability, this was only a small percentage of his business, and we would need to bring it all down to save even more people.

Tenika Vasco of the New York Renegades was descended from Angolan Unbounded, and she'd be more than happy to pose as a slave to infiltrate his operation. Her ability was called hypnosuggestion, and she could talk any but the most resistant to coming around to her way of thinking. Plus, she was a strong soldier, so she'd be safe enough if we kept an eye on her. I didn't like the idea of delaying anything, especially in light of the other people stolen from the North, but that couldn't be helped. Unless I could come up with another plan—and fast.

My thoughts scattered when I realized Frances wasn't waiting where I'd first found her. The tarp was still there, but the tattered bag of belongings was not. Anxiously, I searched the area. Had she found her way to the original escape point?

I leaned over and touched a huddled form, and a man uncurled to look at me. "The woman who was here with her family, a sick little girl. Did you see where she went?"

"No, Massa." When I nodded my thanks, he curled back up and closed his eyes.

"I see her go," a little boy spoke up, rising with a blanket wrapped around his thin shoulders. "With my momma. De boss man take 'em. He havin' a party and need some workers. Her girl wasn't with her."

"He chose Miss Frances?" I knew slavers claimed they could barely tell one slave from another, but it was odd that he'd chosen her when he knew I would be bringing back her child.

"No, she jest follow de others that was taken."

Getting out one way or the other—I had to admire Frances's ingenuity. She must have expected me to leave with Mabel and figured that following the other slaves out of the pen was her only chance to join her family. But escaping on her own put her at higher risk of being caught. I had to get to her before she made the attempt.

I nodded at the child and turned away.

"Massa," he asked, "is my momma comin' back?" He looked frightened as he bent in on himself.

"I think so." For all the good it would do him tomorrow. He looked about Mabel's age and according to law that was old enough for separation.

Swallowing the bitter lump in my throat, I hurried to the wide gate and escaped. Relief filled me as I left the hopelessness and anguish behind.

A whistled signal drew me to the shadows near the rendezvous point, where Ritter waited. In his arms, he cradled Mabel, now wrapped in an additional blanket from our supplies, her face partially covered so no one could see her color.

At the question in his eyes, I shook my head. "Frances is with an Unbounded I met earlier in the courtyard. Name's Cardiff, and apparently Johansson works for him. He's got to be Emporium. We don't have much time." If we were going to save her, I meant, but I wouldn't voice it aloud because of the child, who might not be asleep.

He nodded. "I'll go."

"No. You'd better get her to Locke. She needs attention." I was strong and quick, but Ritter could move faster than any combat Unbounded I'd met, even Eva when she'd been alive. "I'll track down Frances."

The muscles in his jaw worked. Clearly, Ritter wanted to protest but didn't because he knew I was right. I was also his leader, and he knew how to follow a leader he believed in. It was why I could trust him with my life.

He gave a sharp nod. "I'll meet you when I'm finished."

CHAPTER 9

RITTER VANISHED INTO THE NIGHT TO CATCH UP WITH LOCKE and the others, while I exchanged my crate for an oversized bag of weapons and disguises. I had to be prepared for anything. It was barely past the normal dinner hour, but darkness lay heavily on the cold streets.

After a little asking around, I located Cardiff's residence. In typical Emporium fashion—and Renegade as well—he apparently owned a two-story, red-brick house on the south edge of town, using it only when he was here on business. No wonder he needed additional slaves for his event. No doubt he would be entertaining other slavers and local leaders, and the staff who normally kept his house wouldn't be enough for a large event.

Cardiff's house was set back from the road, with a large space for carriage parking, as though he entertained often. A cobblestone walkway, huge white columns, and a second-floor veranda over the entry testified of his wealth and privilege. Bright lights burned from every window, making the house gleam like an evil jack-o'-lantern on All Hallows' Eve, contrasting sharply with the happy, playful music that floated on the cool night air.

Couples had already begun arriving at the house, dressed in their finest clothing. A stableboy directed the drivers where to park after delivering their wealthy cargo, and three drivers already stood in a group near one of the parked carriages, smoking and mumbling in low voices.

I skirted the house, pausing only to look into the windows. I saw white servants dressed in uniforms, arranging platters of food. No slaves there. Apparently Cardiff didn't like his slaves to have direct contact with his guests. I'd have better luck around back.

Sure enough, the kitchens at the rear of the house were alive with activity. A dozen women, their dark faces lean and unsmiling, hurried about their business. Such a contrast from my plantation where laughter often rose over the clatter of pots and pans. Most of the women wore the standard clothing issued by slavers before a sale, but a few wore uniforms and seemed to be directing the others.

None of the women were Frances. Had she already tried to run away? If so, she could be lying in a ditch somewhere, and I was risking her family and myself for nothing by looking for her. I pushed the thoughts to a corner of my mind with the other dark thoughts that haunted my past.

I was debating whether to go in through the back door when a single scream pierced the night, barely distinguishable under the music. It cut off instantly, but the sound had come from the direction of the stables. I ran, keeping to the shadows. Pausing near the barn's partially open double doors, I stashed my bags into some bushes and pushed out my thoughts. No life forces glowed near the entrance, but there were numerous life forces of animals. Deeper inside, I located people. Two, maybe, or three if two of them were very close together. They were deep enough inside the structure that the distance made it difficult to distinguish.

I slid inside, checking my pistol but knowing using it would be a last resort.

The inside of the barn was dim except for a glow at the end of a row of horse stalls. I moved stealthily past the stalls, aware of the animals watching me. I sent out a calming emotion, which generally worked with both animals and mortals. Not so well with Unbounded since they usually blocked their minds.

At the end of the stalls, I reached an open area, dimly illuminated by the light cast from a lantern that was hanging on a nail near a mound of flattened straw. A white male with a worn hat pulled low over his eyes had his arms around a woman with dark skin. She was weeping. Her back was toward me, but I could see her clothing was torn and disheveled, her hair full of straw. Her emotions told me she'd been violated.

Frances!

I launched myself at them, tearing the woman from the man's grasp and throwing my fist into his face, even as a part of my brain registered that the woman wasn't Frances after all.

Pain exploded in my cheek as the man lashed out at me. I'd almost expected Cardiff when I'd first heard the scream, but this man wasn't Unbounded and he dressed like a common slaver. Maybe Johansson then? But wouldn't he be over at his boss's party?

I ducked his next punch, and spun, landing a kick on his thigh that made him cry out. I slammed him twice more, then blocked one jab and took another on the shoulder. Not a hard hit, and it put me into a good position. I pulled back for the finishing blow.

He rushed me, his heavier weight giving him advantage as he knocked me to the straw-carpeted ground. I twisted free as we hit, my hat flying and taking my brown wig with it.

I struck hard before he could manage to pin me. Something in his face gave, and blood spurted between us. I jumped to my feet while he was still on his knees and pressed forward, punching hard and taking another blow, so I could whip around and put him in a headlock. My chin knocked his hat to the ground.

"Move and you die," I growled, pressing my knife against his throat.

"Stop!" the woman shouted. "Stop!"

I looked to my side to see her grabbing a pitch fork, then twirling it so the prongs pointed at my head.

"What?" I said, not relinquishing my hold. "I'm trying to save you!"

The woman jabbed the pitchfork closer. "He saved me!" she said at the same moment the man asked, "*You're trying to save her?*"

I craned my neck to see the man's face. His eyes, now unhidden by his hat, stared back at me, bright blue and familiar. "You!" I whispered, my hold loosening. Gone were the expensive clothes, and he'd definitely done something to fake that hair sprouting from his face because he'd been clean-shaven in the hotel dining room only a few hours ago.

"You seem to have me at a disadvantage," he said, his voice teasing as it had been at the hotel, as though the entire brawl had amused him. "Whom do I have the pleasure of addressing?"

I was relieved he didn't recognize me, though my hat was gone and my blond hair, pinned tightly to my head, was obviously more abundant than that of a typical male. Before I could respond, I became aware of another life force behind several bales of hay. Two life forces, I had thought when I'd entered the barn, but the man and woman had been too close and I should have counted them separately. The other life force was lying motionless but still burning strong.

The man's eyes flicked over to the bale, following my stare. "I see you located the real perpetrator."

I blinked because he couldn't possibly know that I could sense the unconscious man behind the hay.

Could he? Then I spied a boot emerging from behind the bale; it had to be what the man thought had drawn my attention.

"I assume that means there's a man attached to that boot," I said, still using a deep voice that I hoped would continue to hide my identity despite the loss of my hat and wig. "All right. I'm going to step back now."

"Please do," he said dryly. To the woman, he added, "I think you can put that down now."

She nodded, her eyes bulging slightly, and lowered the pitchfork but didn't drop it entirely. Who could blame her?

In a swift move, I released the man and stood, still gripping the knife just in case, placing him between me and the pitchfork. He arose, removed a handkerchief from his pocket, and began wiping the blood from his face. He was taller than I was, though not by much, but he had a good thirty pounds on me, at least. Even with the disguise, he was attractive, and I didn't like the way something in me reacted to him.

"Who are you?" I asked.

One brow arched. "Who are you?"

Mortals were so tedious at times. I hoped I wouldn't have to knock them both out and remove their memories before I could continue looking for Frances. "You first," I said, pulling out my pistol, though I had no intention of using it and alerting those in the house to my presence.

"Hold it," he said, his hands out in front of him. "I am here only because I heard Lucias Johansson illegally enslaved free Negroes. I plan to stop him, so I talked to a few people I know, found out where he was, and followed him to the house. I was waiting for my contacts when he took a liking to this woman"—he dipped his head respectfully in her direction—"and I had to take action." To her, he added. "I'm sorry I wasn't able to stop him sooner." He was telling the truth on both accounts, I sensed.

"Then we are essentially on the same side." I put away the gun.

The woman gave a sob, her face crumpling. "I want to go home to my family." Finally, she let go of the pitchfork.

"Are you from the North?" I asked. She sounded younger than I'd first thought. Not a woman, really, but a girl. It was hard to tell sometimes when children often worked in the fields under the hot sun. Whatever her former occupation, she was both pretty and curvaceous, which was probably why Johansson had targeted her.

She shook her head. "Petersburg."

Virginia. A slave, ripped from her family. Not illegally. Her emotions were all over the place, and I had to block them before the despair made me desperate.

The man averted his gaze, taking a step in my direction and reaching out a hand. "You can call me Smith." For the first time he was telling me an untruth, but as I wasn't about to share my identity, I didn't hold it against him. If I needed, I could get it from his thoughts, but more pressing matters demanded my attention.

Ignoring his outstretched hand and the way his smile

made my heart trip harder in my chest, I stepped around the bale of hay to look at the sprawled man. His pants were on, but sagging around his hips, his untucked shirt hiding most of him. He was obviously out for the count.

"So this is Johansson," I mused. He was dressed for a party. Not nearly as nicely as his more dangerous boss, but he clearly wasn't hurting for cash. No wonder, if he was abducting people from the North.

"My plan," Smith came up beside me, "was to have him arrested tonight, and when I learned about the party, I thought the more witnesses the better. But after this"—his head indicated the inert figure—"I may be the one who ends up in jail." He meant because the slave girl was Johansson's property, and if he wanted to molest her, it was his business in most men's eyes. Not in Smith's, though. I warmed a little more toward him and mentally cursed the fact that we'd run into each other like this instead of tomorrow at the hotel.

"He'll never remember you." I stepped across Johansson's body and squatted on his other side where I could still keep an eye on Smith and the girl. "Make sure no one is coming," I told Smith. Finding a liquor flask in Johansson's pocket, I unscrewed the cap and began splashing him with the contents. No one else was approaching, of course, or I'd sense a new life force, but I didn't want Smith to see what I was going to do next.

Smith obeyed me with that amused glint in his eyes, one that for some reason made me want to jump into his mind and discover his secrets. But I didn't invade people without a reason, especially good people, and I believed he was honorable.

Placing my hand on Johansson's head, I pushed into his mind. Unconscious thoughts were much less volatile than conscious ones. No sand stream of rushing thoughts, just a placid lake. I dove into it. Down, down—until I saw bubbles of thoughts. Not everyone's unconscious state represented as a lake, but most did, and I was glad he was typical.

Stepping aside from an oncoming bubble, I began searching for the one that held memory of this night. There. Dragging the girl to the barn, his body burning with anticipation, the girl's struggle heightening his lust. Her soft, warm flesh as he felt her breasts through the cloth and pushed aside her skirts. Her scream as he pushed her down and forced her legs apart. Then outrage as he was yanked to his feet, his lust not yet fully satisfied.

I plucked the entire bubble, pulling it to me until it disappeared. I didn't know or care where it went, but for him it no longer existed. I took the next one, too, where, after a few furious blows, Smith's fist plunged him into blackness.

Disgusted, I opened my eyes to see the girl watching me. "I'm sorry," I whispered, for her ears only.

A heavy single tear dripped from her eye and skidded down her cheek. "Not the first time. I had a baby once."

I saw in her thoughts the rest she didn't say, that she'd only been twelve and her mulatto son had died at birth.

I wanted to castrate Johansson right then, and every other male slave owner for good measure. Or take all his memories so that he'd be as helpless as a baby. Only Frances stopped me from taking the time, because I'd seen her in his mind, along with the rest when they arrived with Cardiff. She was in the house and that meant, one way or the other, I had to go inside and free her.

I arose. "We need you to keep quiet about our being here," I said, keeping my voice gentle. "Get back to the house. Not a word."

Her eyes fell to Johansson. "He'll kill me when he wakes."

"He won't remember, I swear to you. I have this." I reached inside my jacket and down my shirt, pulling out the small talisman nestled between my breasts. It had been carved back in 1755 by the oldest slave on the Savannah plantation. At the time, I'd been with Wymon and Eva for ten years. Ten years since I'd murdered Simon, and my nightmares had disrupted the household. The slave told me it was African magic and that it would make the nightmares stop. They did stop, and though I was sure it was more because of his kindness than any magic, I'd carried the talisman with me on missions ever since.

The girl's soft gasp told me she believed in magic. This would be more understandable to her than my own ability, which I supposed could be viewed as a magic of sorts instead of an inborn skill.

"Go on," I said. She nodded and hurried into the darkness past Smith. I stood as he abandoned his watch and strode in my direction. He carried a dark bag I hadn't seen before.

"A little alcohol isn't going to stop Johansson from remembering what I did to him," he said. "And if I don't go into that party and give my people the signal when he finally wakes from his sweet dreams, he won't be arrested and the people he kidnapped will be sold as slaves."

"If you clean up, he won't recognize you." I almost added, "I didn't," but stopped myself. "But at this point, I'm not sure you should do anything. Johansson isn't calling the shots anymore, if he ever was. Some man called Cardiff is in charge."

"The man who owns this place." He shrugged, his expression hardening. "Doesn't matter. If he knows that Johansson has been abducting free people, he should be arrested as well."

His eager righteousness was admirable, but he knew nothing of the Emporium and their viciousness. If they couldn't free their agent by bribery or force, they'd simply fake a death and move him elsewhere. A shot through the head might hurt Cardiff temporarily, but he'd awake to do more damage within days.

"You don't understand," I said. "Cardiff is dangerous. You stay away from him. He's *my* problem."

Smith's eyes regarded me unwaveringly. Even in the dim light, I could see their color, but I didn't recognize his expression, and for once, his emotions, though I could feel them, were unclear. My heartbeat increased.

"All right," he said finally. "You can have Cardiff

while I'll take on this clown." He thumbed down at Johansson. "I'll go in the house and make sure it's all set up." He dropped his bag and began unbuttoning his shirt.

"What are you doing?" I asked, as it dropped to the ground.

"Well, I can't go in looking like this."

He had a nice wide chest, covered with curly blond hair that beckoned to be touched. I didn't avert my gaze. Unbounded weren't concerned with nudity the way most mortals were. Something about living two thousand years and fighting in close combat often made it necessary for us to disrobe in front of our comrades, regardless of gender. I'd seen Ritter and many others in various stages of dress without reaction.

I was reacting now.

Okay, maybe it wasn't only the idea of having children that stopped my last relationship. Maybe it ended because I didn't have these feelings. I had cared for my suitor, had enjoyed his kisses, but I'd never wanted to lose myself in him. Never wanted to tell him about my past or my true self. I'd begun to wonder if Simon had forever ruined the part of me that made me a woman.

Except at the moment, that part was working overtime. I stood there shocked, whether because that kind of emotion had returned at all or because it was so powerful, I couldn't decide.

Smith pulled on a white silk shirt and began removing his boots. "Maybe you ought to keep watch. I won't be a minute." Again his voice was teasing, as though it didn't bother him that another man was staring at him as he dressed. Maybe he liked men in that way. But, no, I'd felt his attraction to me earlier.

Remember Frances, I told myself, stepping across Johansson, who, as if by signal, jerked. Not conscious yet, but it wouldn't be long.

I stopped to get my hat and wig, and by the time I reached the dark corridor between the horse stalls, my mind was working on a plan. My own clothing would need to be adjusted in order to get me inside the house undetected by Cardiff. Or maybe a different disguise altogether. He'd probably remember the physician's assistant with the scar. I had everything I needed in one of my bags.

I told myself I was going in for Frances, but I knew it was also for Smith. He might be man enough to take down Johansson, but I'd barely broken a sweat immobilizing him, and that meant Cardiff could easily kill Smith and his contacts. I wished Ritter at least were here, but hopefully the surprise on my side would allow me to handle a lone Emporium agent.

If there was only one.

Smith looked like a new man as he approached me in a burgundy tailcoat with a deep V opening that revealed his shirt and a dark cravat that matched the snug pants. Only his face looked odd with spots of the face paint that he was attempting to scrub off with his bloody handkerchief.

"I will let you know what happens," he said. "But tell me, is all this off my face?"

"No. Here." I pointed to my own face to show him where. "I'm going inside with you."

His eyes fell over my clothes. "I went to a lot of trouble to obtain an invitation, but they won't let you in like that, even if I vouch for you."

"I have other clothes. No, not there—you're missing it." I pulled out my own handkerchief and scrubbed off his cheek near his ear. This close he was even more compelling. "There." I gave him my handkerchief, feeling heated under his stare.

"You really intend to accompany me?"

"I have supplies outside. Just give me a few minutes."

"All right. But I must tell you that you are losing something." His hand went to my face and pinched, pulling off a large piece of my fake scar.

Oh, no. The piece kept coming. When he'd hit me earlier, it must have broken lose. The next thing I knew his other hand was on my chin and the realistic beard stubble Locke had worked so hard on came away.

Realization changed his expression to one of surprise. "Why you're . . . not a man at all!" He laughed, a glad sound that was unexpected in this dark place. "The woman from the hotel! I thought you seemed familiar. Your eyes. I've never seen gray that color before."

My cover was blown, but maybe I didn't need it anymore. Maybe in this case no disguise was the best disguise. Without responding, I turned and started toward the barn doors. Steps from behind told me he intended to come along.

I retrieved my bag, and we went back inside the barn, though not past the stalls this time. Rummaging inside the bag, I pushed a canteen filled with water at him. "You still have blood on your forehead."

It probably said something about his character that, though I could sense he urgently wanted to, he didn't once look my way as I traded my pants and shirt for a blush rose gown with a pointed waist and sloping shoulders. It had been packed tightly in one of my bags, but the material was impervious to wrinkles, or impervious enough not to attract notice. The neckline showed a good deal more cleavage than my usual choice, but left me freedom to fight. I didn't use a corset, of course, as that would have hindered movement. The gown had been specifically designed in England by our Renegade allies to hide weapons—mostly knives and a short sword, of which I was rather proud.

Brushing out my hair, I swept it up into something that would be appropriate for a party. I used a solution to wipe off the rest of my disguise, and my small mirror revealed that I hadn't escaped my fight with Smith unscathed. Under where the fake scar had been, my chin sported a large bruise that was fading fast, and a cut on my lip was knitting itself back together. I had other bruises on my body, but only the one on my shoulder showed slightly. A little face paint would hide all the damage well enough, especially if I let another fifteen minutes pass. Before the hour was out, I'd be completely healed.

I mentally checked on Johansson, then hurried toward the barn door where Smith waited. "Time to leave. He'll be awake any minute."

Smith's eyes widened, and it did something inside me to feel the tug of his desire as he regarded my new self. "I have just one question," he said, his voice strangely husky.

"I might answer." I thought he would ask my identity, or how I'd become involved with abolitionists—none of which I could tell him.

"Where did you learn to fight like that?"

Ah, now I detected a bit of wounded pride. I laughed. "Around."

I tried to move past him, but he remained motionless, his eyes still locked on my face. "Your bruise. It's gone."

"You just can't see it. It's dark." We had left the lantern with Johansson at the other end of the barn, but Smith was apparently seeing enough.

His gaze dropped to the cut on my lip, though he couldn't possibly see it under the red I'd painted there. My Unbounded genes boiled, demanding that I take what I wanted. What I'd been thinking of since the moment I'd seen his chest. Two steps would be all I'd need to get closer to him. I wouldn't have to raise myself far to meet his lips.

He dragged his eyes back to mine, and they echoed the passion that had sprung between us, heavy and aching.

I was lost. I hadn't expected this reaction in myself. Yes, the Unbounded gene was driven to survival, and I'd learned to control simple urges, but this was different.

No, this was a mistake. I stepped past him. "Johansson's waking."

"But—"

"Hurry."

"Who are you?" he asked, his voice still rough.

"You can call me Ava."

CHAPTER 10

I DON'T KNOW WHY I TOLD HIM MY REAL NAME, NOT THAT it mattered. Only those closest to me knew it now. Everyone else was dead. *As this mortal will be,* I told myself, *before you age another year.* Getting attached was never without risks and consequences.

I needed to focus on Frances.

We walked around to the front of the house. Several servants stared at us as we strode up the walk, but Smith winked at them and gave me a heated look that they couldn't misinterpret. I laughed. At least my new persona gave Smith a reason to be skulking around Cardiff's house. They would likely assume we had arrived earlier but had taken the opportunity for a little sport before going inside.

At the door, Smith handed the white butler an invitation. So many life forces were already present, glowing in my mind as bright as the oil lanterns placed to enhance the gas lighting installed in the house. We were ushered into a large parlor where no expense had been spared. The evidence of opulence was everywhere, from the handmade lace tablecloths to the rare foods on the banquet table. I could see no life forces blocking my mental searches, and the resulting jumble of emotions and thoughts was insane. So many in this room were angry, ambitious, and eager.

The mental cacophony would have overwhelmed me years ago, but now I cataloged, assessed, and blocked the people who were of no concern. As I'd seen before, only white servants were present in this room. Their master was nowhere to be seen.

"Is that ice cream?" Smith asked.

I sensed he loved the stuff. "So it appears." I gave him a level stare and he colored slightly. "Are your friends here?"

He nodded. "I've given them the signal. They'll act when Johansson arrives."

I followed his eyes to the side of the room holding the refreshment table. A man with a sheriff's badge stood with four other men. Not many against an Unbounded. Unless they were trained by someone like Locke or Ritter.

Where was Cardiff?

I pushed out my thoughts, searching for both Cardiff and Frances. I wished my ability weren't limited by distance, but I had to work with what I was given. I moved across the room, and Smith went with me. Eyes followed us, a customary occurrence. Mortals saw the undisguised me as far more than beautiful. Striking, perhaps. Compelling. It no longer fazed me—except Smith's sudden reluctance to leave my side, which could get him killed.

"Attend to your friends," I said. "I have my own agenda."

He gave me a wink. "I'll go talk with them, but I'm not finished with you, Miss Ava. Don't forget that I know where you are staying."

So much promise and confidence in his voice. He must have enjoyed the benefits of a good education, and I wondered what he did for a profession. Perhaps some kind of law enforcement. If he survived this night, I might find out.

Something in me shifted at that thought. If Smith died, it would be at the hands of Cardiff because I had failed. I needed backup if I wanted to have more than a chance of getting Smith and Frances out of here in one piece. Not to mention all the party guests. Ritter should arrive soon, unless he and Locke had encountered difficulties. I prayed that they hadn't.

Refusing a drink proffered by a servant, I slipped into the hallway, acting as if I knew where I was going. One servant stared at me as she passed with a new platter of ice cream, but I ignored her.

I reached the kitchen, but I couldn't find Frances, not even in alcoves and corners that I hadn't been able to see from the outside. Near the fireplace, the girl Smith had rescued in the barn looked up at me and then away again quickly, as though hoping not to be noticed. That made two of us, though she couldn't possibly recognize me in my present dress.

I stopped one of the slaves, whose clothing told me she'd come from the Forks of the Road. "I'm looking for Frances. Do you know where she is?"

She shook her head. "Maybe upstairs. We was told to make up rooms for the guests."

"Thank you." With the size of this group, it made sense that some of the guests would be staying. I only hoped Cardiff didn't make an appearance before I found her.

I'd only gone a few feet down the hall when a side door banged open, and there was Johansson, looking more confused than angry. He had a cut on his forehead, which he'd tried unsuccessfully to clean, instead smearing his face with blood.

"You there!" he growled at the servant who had passed me earlier with the ice cream platter. "I need attention." His eyes met mine as several white servants clustered around him, one with a basket of supplies.

I turned, feeling his eyes digging into me, and made my way down the hall to warn Smith about his arrival and to ask him to hold off on confronting Johansson until I found Frances. As I entered the parlor, Cardiff loomed before me. I recognized him instantly, though his clothing was considerably more elegant than it had been at the Forks of the Road.

His attention immediately fell to me, and a smile slashed across his handsome face, this time minus the cruelty. He bowed without apparent recognition. "Good evening. I am John Cardiff, your host. I am delighted to meet you Miss . . ."

"Mrs. Smith," I said, with a curtsy. "Frances Smith. The pleasure is mine. I am a visitor to your city. I came with my husband, who is probably over by the ice cream." I let admiration creep into my tone at the mention of the treat, a sentiment I was far from feeling.

"I am glad he is enjoying himself." He took my hand, though I had not offered, bringing it to his lips without releasing my eyes. "As this is not my usual residence and I come here only on business, fate must be smiling upon me to have our paths cross this enchanting evening. I trust you found what you were looking for?" He was asking my reason for wandering around his house, which showed that despite his glib words, he was suspicious of everyone. As he should be.

I was.

"Indeed," I replied. "I had a mishap with your ice cream, but it has been resolved." I touched my bare neck and his eyes greedily followed the motion before slipping lower. Maybe it wouldn't be so hard to trap this Emporium agent despite his caution—as long as he was alone. A little distraction would give me ample opportunity.

Besides craving for power and a blatant contempt for mortal life, another way Emporium Unbounded were not like Renegades was in their view of family. For Unbounded, intimacy always meant having children, as the Unbounded gene sought reproduction, and children meant the responsibility of checking up on them and their descendants for six generations to see if any posterity underwent the Change. Or for much longer if new Unbounded blood entered the family line. Renegades guarded family and relationships fiercely. We didn't dally. We loved with all we were until death, or we stayed apart. It was our way.

The Emporium was more like the parasitic cuckoo, planting their offspring where someone else would have to deal with the consequences until the child came of age. In their disregard for mortals, they viewed them as incubators and nannies to increase their own strength. In that light, a dalliance with a married woman was often most practical for their intentions. No one to kill or to pay off. No responsibility.

"Excuse me." I inclined my head and moved away, a little too fast for courtesy, but wise because my survival instincts were pushing me to attack this dangerous enemy. That had to wait until I found Frances.

I sidled up to Smith, who looked more pleased to see me than he should. "Johansson's here," I murmured, "but so is Cardiff, and I still haven't found the person I'm looking for."

"Oh?" His brow arched again in a way that for some unknown reason made my chest ache. "I didn't know you were looking for someone."

"I am. That's why I need you to hold off. I have to make sure she's safe."

His eyes went past me. "Too late." His voice held an apology.

There in the doorway to the parlor stood Johansson, looking like a man completely out of his element. Unlike Cardiff, he would be more comfortable with the servants rather than among this group of Natchez elite, regardless of his finery. The men Smith had pointed out earlier had already begun talking to him. I moved closer to hear what they were saying.

"What I'm saying is that we have proof that you have abducted free Negroes from the North," said the man with the badge. "Do you deny this?"

Johansson's already ruddy face grew more flushed. "I most certainly do. Tell me, where are my accusers?"

"Here." Smith stepped forward, pulling out a paper. "I have an official complaint drawn up by Wellison and Durham, attorneys at law, who have evidence to support the accusation."

"I . . . well . . . that ain't possible," blustered Johansson. Guilt radiated from him like a foul stench but was overshadowed by anger. "I am a respected businessman. I have paperwork for all my slaves."

"Then you won't mind presenting it," Smith said with a little smirk. "But the complaint involves more than your current batch of slaves. Wellison and Durham would like to investigate your files for evidence of past abuses."

Wellison and Durham—why did that name seem familiar?

Cardiff stepped close to Smith and took the paper, perusing it briefly before crumpling it in his hand. "This is preposterous! Johansson works for me and to accuse him is to accuse me. My reputation is indisputable. You have only to query the governor of Virginia to ascertain whether or not this case has merit."

Interesting. That meant the Emporium had someone in the governor's office, if not the governor himself, who was Unbounded or working for them. When this was over, I would make it a point to find out who and eliminate them. For now it meant that forged papers would likely come from the governor's office and Johansson would walk away free.

The sheriff hesitated, holding his handcuffs uncertainly. Smith glared at him. "You can't wait. Miss Amelia Mitchell, a respected plantation owner in Georgia, has lodged a complaint in a legal manner. Let these men present proof of their ownership immediately if they have any."

My stomach did a little twist. Amelia Mitchell. Oh, yes, I knew that name—too well—but what I didn't know is how Smith had heard it. He believed he was telling the truth, I sensed, but he couldn't be unless . . . *Oh, no.*

There was only one way I could think of that would explain both his involvement and my immediate attraction to him. No wonder Wellison and Durham seemed so familiar.

"You come to my home as a guest and dare question me?" Cardiff put a hand on his hip, though I couldn't see the pistols that had been there earlier.

Smith's frown deepened. "If that's what it takes. I believe the law will prevail."

Cardiff's hand went to a bulge in his coat, which was probably exactly what I thought it was. I stepped in front of Smith, wishing I had known of his connections before we entered this house. I might have played the game differently.

"He is only saying that Mr. Johansson must have worked to deceive everyone," I said. To the sheriff, I added, "Johansson does have free Negroes in his possession. I know this because I paid for their release and sent them to the North myself. They must be freed. That is why I am here tonight."

A collective gasp went up from the guests. A complaint by someone not present held little weight compared to a live witness, especially a white, obviously well-to-do witness. I was acutely aware of Smith behind me, whose shock was greater than anyone's.

I didn't dare look away from Cardiff's narrowed eyes. I'd given him a way out, a way to put the blame on Johansson. But would he take it? Forty slaves and a look into past sales meant a considerable sum, but even if they uncovered hundreds of violations, this setback would mean relatively nothing to him. He had centuries to amass untold wealth.

His nostrils flared and anger briefly exploded from his

mind, then disappeared just as suddenly as he controlled himself. I suspected the anger meant he wasn't going to end this peacefully, but what remained to be discovered was if I could beat him. The Emporium were known for breeding combat Unbounded, and if that was his ability, my focus would be more a question of holding out until Ritter arrived than beating Cardiff myself. I had prepared for something like this confrontation the entire past century, but he might have also.

Outside, a sudden wind rattled the windows. An unnatural wind. The concentration on Cardiff's face was unmistakable.

Maybe my chances of besting him weren't so bad after all.

CHAPTER 11

Even as I had the thought, the storm outside grew stronger. People stared at each other in confusion and worry. Two women and three men hurried to the windows. Murmurs started, and at least one woman fainted and had to be carried to a couch. Only Cardiff smiled, his eyes holding mine, his face arrogant and self-assured.

Assured as I was when I took someone's memories or felt their emotions.

"Perhaps," Cardiff said to the sheriff, "it would be wise to take this up another day. It appears there is a severe storm gathering." As if to punctuate his words, the entire house shook.

I alone realized that it wasn't just a chance storm. I'd heard of an Emporium agent with the ability to manipulate wind. He had caused us many deaths over the years, but we'd never identified the Unbounded with the gift.

Until now.

"Like the tornado five years ago!" a woman cried out. "Oh, dear. I have to get home to the children!" She grabbed her husband's hand and hurried out of the parlor, heading toward the entryway.

Amusement filled Cardiff's eyes. "I think it would be wise if we all secured our homes."

Smith moved around me and lunged toward Johansson. "He'll be coming with us, then."

A sword suddenly blocked his way. "I think not." Cardiff's smile mocked us. I hadn't seen him grab the sword, but I wasn't surprised he had one. All Unbounded carried them close these days.

"Mr. Cardiff is right," said the sheriff, retreating with his companions toward the entry. "We can deal with Mr. Johansson later. If it's anything like that tornado five years ago, we have far more important things to concern us."

More important than a stolen life, he meant. Because after all, the people I was trying to free were considered only a subspecies, while a tornado might kill whites. His implication made me furious despite the very real threat Cardiff represented.

The house rattled again more violently as guests hurried toward the entryway, many without pausing for their outerwear. I knew why. The tornado of 1840 had come just as suddenly, and more than three hundred lives had been lost, with numerous boats, plantations, and dwellings destroyed. The total deaths in reality were rumored to have been much higher because slave deaths often went unreported.

Smith retreated from the sword but returned immediately with a poker he'd grabbed from the fireplace. Johansson cowered behind Cardiff. "Now, now," said the sheriff, "we will settle this later."

I had to admire Smith's courage, even though he was ultimately not a match for Cardiff.

From outside there was a huge crash and several women closest to me screamed and tried to force their way into the growing crowd spilling from the parlor into the entryway. At the same time, slave women flooded in from the back hallway where I'd gone looking for Frances earlier. Their eyes were wide with terror, and a few of the younger ones sobbed. I spied Frances among them and gladness spread through me. I would take her to her family, and tomorrow Smith and I could worry about the others.

"What do we do, Massa?" a slave asked Johansson.

"Git out of here!" Johansson spat. A stream of curses followed as he lashed out at the nearest woman, who shrank away from him.

In the midst of the slaves, I spotted the girl from the barn at the same time she saw Smith. Keeping as far from Johansson as she could, she ran toward us. "Please, the servants say we're goin' t' die!"

Smith had already begun moving toward her when

Cardiff leapt forward, his sword singing through the air. Time seemed to slow as I turned, watching it slice with amazing precision.

Smith! I thought.

My own short sword was abruptly in my hands, and I moved to counter, even as the sword struck the slave girl. The blade sliced through her neck, coming out the other side. She took another step before her head rolled off her shoulders and her body collapsed. Her life force vanished.

Horrified screams echoed from both the whites and the slaves.

"Get back to the kitchens!" Cardiff shouted at the slaves. "Go, you filthy, blood-sucking wretches! You belong to me, and if you don't leave now I'll slaughter the lot of you!"

The crowd of whites looked toward the sheriff and his men, but we all knew there wasn't a court in the land that would convict Cardiff, especially if his Virginia contacts could provide evidence that the girl had been in cahoots with abolitionists.

With a great swelling, the slaves and the guests fled from both sides of the room, until only Cardiff, Johansson, Smith, and I remained. Several heartbeats passed as the wind howled and banged at the windows.

Cardiff smiled and raised his sword toward Smith.

This time I was there first, blocking him, move for move. He was good, but I'd been trained by better. His attention was also on the wind, as he controlled and manipulated it.

"Renegade," he said with a sneer.

I smiled. "Took you long enough to figure it out."

His only answer was a knife that sailed toward Smith where he grappled with Johansson. The knife dug into Smith's shoulder and he cried out. Johansson took the opportunity to scurry away, but Smith tripped him with the poker and jumped on him, fists pumping.

Cardiff laughed, and outside the storm grew louder. He fumbled for another weapon inside the folds of his coat, but this time I stopped him with my own throwing knife. I'd always been rather good, but I missed his throat by several inches, partially embedding the knife instead in his upper chest. Not a fatal wound, unfortunately, but one that would slow him down.

He swiped at the knife, pulling it out, then attacked with fervency, as though determined to beat me back with sheer determination and the larger size of his sword. But he was tiring. I just had to play it out long enough to let his wounds and his efforts with the storm weaken him further. From the corner of my eye, I could see that Smith was on top of Johansson, tying his hands behind his back. In a moment he'd be free to help me with Cardiff.

Or maybe to get in the way.

From the back hallway, I sensed another life force approaching the parlor. Reaching out, I saw Frances—and that she gripped a heavy cast iron frying pan in her stiff hands. I needed to end this dance before either she or Smith were hurt.

"Hold!" Cardiff sidestepped my lunge. "Truce," he said. "I let you and this mortal go free. I'll also stop the wind." Not stupid, he had come to the same conclusion I had about his likelihood of beating me.

I gave a very unladylike snort. "That's assuming I believe you, which I don't." With a series of furious blows, I had him scrambling backwards. "And assuming this *mortal* means something to me, which he doesn't." This I said so he wouldn't waste energy killing Smith. The sentiments, though not typically Renegade, should be close enough to his own to be believed.

"Then the whole town dies!" Cardiff shouted.

Wind exploded the windows, punching into the room and stealing my breath. The doors banged open and then shut and open again. The pins ripped from my hair, throwing the strands across my vision. My skirts billowed and wrapped around my legs. Pictures flew off the wall, lanterns fell over, food sailed through the air. The wind screamed and howled liked damned souls in hell, and I had to fight not to clap my hands over my ears.

Yet I noticed the flames from the oil lamps blew out before they could light anything on fire and the heavier furniture stayed in place. Whatever else he did, Cardiff planned on saving his house.

I glanced toward Smith and saw with relief that he was holding his own. Relief because I did care very much about him; I'd been caring about him and his family for over a hundred years.

The violent turbulence eased slightly as Cardiff again went for the weapon in his coat. I was faster. Despite the wind, my pistol rang out, the ball flying true and clear to carve a hole in his forehead. He toppled forward, missing Smith and Johansson by a few inches.

Instantly, the wind ceased.

I reached out mentally, searching for Frances. She was still in the hallway, frightened and hugging the ground, if the glow from her life force was any indicator, but she was not in any pain.

Dropping the pistol, I stepped closer to Cardiff, raising my sword in both hands. *Never again.* He was too dangerous to let regenerate.

"What are you doing!" Smith yelled, jumping to his feet and grabbing my hands. "He's already dead."

"No, he's not!" I shouted. "And if I *don't* do this, you and everyone in this town will be dead before the week is over."

"What are you talking about?" His face was close to mine, his eyes disbelieving.

"The wind—listen! It's gone. It was him! I know you don't understand it, but believe me when I say he was responsible. He's not going to sit back while we take what he sees as his property. He'll make sure everyone pays. In fact, your sheriff and his friends are already as good as dead if I don't do this. Now let me go!"

Horror filled Smith's face. Whether because he

believed me, or because he decided I was crazy, I wasn't sure. He released me and stepped back. I brought the sword down hard, slicing through Cardiff's neck and severing it. Blood spilled onto the ground. One focus point to go and he'd never be coming back.

As I moved into position, my foot sent his head rolling to a nearby couch, where the slave girl's head had been wedged by the wind. My stomach roiled. It was my fault she was dead. Mine and Smith's. If we had never gone to the barn, she might still be alive.

I raised the sword again, but in the next instant hands were taking it from me. Ritter. I recognized his emotions of fury and regret—surface emotions he let me see.

"I'll take it from here," he said in my ear. Now his surface emotions were gone, tucked behind the block in his mind with the rest that was buried too deeply for me to ever glimpse. Maybe I never wanted to.

I relinquished the sword because cutting through a man's torso was far more difficult and Ritter was better equipped than I was, both in strength and weaponry. "What took you so long?" I said.

"Ran into a minor complication with some other slavers. Locke is still finishing up." His eyes took in the room. "Not as complicated as here, it appears."

I shrugged. "I found Frances."

Finally a hint of a smile. "Never doubted that you would. Who's he?" He jerked his head at Smith.

"An ally of sorts. Don't kill him." This last I said only half-jokingly.

"Maybe you'd better get him out of here then." Ritter sounded deadly serious. I laughed.

Smith was hauling Johansson to his feet as we talked. I sensed he wasn't happy about my exchange with Ritter, but sometimes with Ritter it was better safe than sorry. Because if Ritter thought for even a second that Smith was a danger, he would kill him without thinking twice about it.

"Stay here," Smith said to Johansson, shoving the man into a chair. Then he turned to me. "This must be the guy from your letter." His gaze flicked over Ritter, his eyes hard.

"Letter?" I had no idea what Smith was talking about.

His tone relaxed and the hint of amusement was back, which impressed me quite a bit with Ritter still glaring in his direction. "My competition," Smith explained. "The man who wrote that letter you were reading so intently at the hotel."

"Oh, that letter." I wanted to laugh at the absurdity. "No, this is a colleague of mine. We work, uh, in the Underground Railroad together. About the letter. There's something—"

At that moment Johansson jumped to his feet and ran for one of the windows, throwing himself through it. With an exclamation, Smith sprang after him.

I sighed. "Well, go on," I told Ritter, nodding at Cardiff's body.

"Hadn't you better go after them?"

"Johansson's hands are tied. Smith should be able to

take care of himself." The words didn't exactly match my feelings about him, but Cardiff was too dangerous to ignore. As the leader of our little band of Renegades, my duty was clear: I had to take care of him now.

I readied the black bag from the supplies Ritter had brought, while he made sure Cardiff was permanently dead. Afterward, I went to find Frances. It took time convincing her the danger was past and to pry the frying pan from her hand, but that was just as well. When I returned with her to the parlor, Cardiff's remains were already packed away. Ritter had also found a blanket and placed it over the slave woman, her head lying where it would have been in life. Sometimes he surprised me.

Blood stained the floor and the scent was overwhelming, but my stomach didn't heave. A tight numbness had filled me, which was almost as bad because it reminded me of my baby. Of losing Wymon and Eva. How many times would I have to battle evil in my very long lifetime? And if I didn't fight it, who would? As long as the Emporium existed, Renegades were the only force standing between them and the enslavement of all mortals, regardless of the color of their skin.

"I'll make them pay for what they did to her," Ritter's voice grated against my ears.

He thought he was referring to the dead girl, but I knew he really meant it for the woman he was to have married. He carried her ring and those of his mother and little sister on a gold chain around his neck. He was never without it.

"Don't blame yourself," I told him. "Neither of us could have stopped it." I let a few seconds go by before adding, "And we both know that death is not the worst thing a person can suffer." Saying it somehow eased the numb feeling in my chest.

He didn't reply, and I had no idea if the words had helped him, but I would keep at it. Someday I would get through. And someday he would find another reason besides revenge to give his life purpose. I knew because I was finally ready to find another reason for myself.

Smith came in then, the proper way through the door, pushing a bruised Johansson in front of him. Smith bent momentarily to peek under the blanket at the slave girl, his mouth set grimly. I wanted to tell him it wasn't really his fault, but I knew it wouldn't help.

"I need to take Johansson to the sheriff," Smith said, "but I have no idea what I'm going to say about Cardiff." His chin jerked toward the black bag at Ritter's feet, which looked more like a bundle of laundry than the remains of a man, though clearly Smith deduced the contents. The bag wouldn't leak, but the blood already on the floor and the disarray caused by the wind made the place gruesome.

"There isn't going to be any reporting of anything," I said. "Cardiff was one of ours"—so to speak—"and he's our responsibility. The local authorities wouldn't have been able to hold him long anyway." It wasn't the time to explain the politics of Unbounded to him, or how they manipulated the mortal world.

Smith regarded me for several quiet seconds. "Okay, I can live with that. What about him?" He glanced over at where Johansson stared dejectedly at the blood-stained floor. "He saw it all. I still need to take him in so I can free some of the people he's taken. But he's bound to talk."

"He's coming with us," Ritter said.

I nodded. "And his so-called cargo. All of it."

Smith stared, and Johansson looked unnerved. "You can't do that!" Johansson growled. "They're mine."

"Not anymore," I said. "You lost that right—if it ever was one—the minute you began abducting free people."

"They ain't people!" he roared.

I nodded at Ritter, and with a blurred motion, he crossed the room and slammed Johansson against the wall, a knife at his throat.

I moved closer until my face was near Johansson's. "Listen and listen good. I'm only going to say this once. They are people, and you will never own or sell another one again. Ever. I will know if you do, just as I know about the many times you've abused and forced yourself on their women, and the fact that your own grandmother was a slave."

He gasped at that and pulled away from me into Ritter's knife. Three beads of blood sprang up along the edge of the blade. "If you so much as raise another hand against a Negro for any reason," I continued, "I'm sending Ritter here after you. Now where are your papers for the people you've got up at the Forks of the Road? You're going to set every man, woman, and child free, or

I will kill you myself. Like I did Cardiff. But without the bullet. And far more slowly."

He nodded, eyes wild, his entire body shaking. Ritter released him with a hint of disappointment.

"Time to leave," I announced.

"My family?" Frances asked.

I smiled. "They're waiting for you on the boat."

Without apparent effort, Ritter hefted the black bag like so much garbage, his stare still pinning Johansson to the wall. Then he grabbed Johansson and pushed him in the direction of the entryway.

"The boat will only fit twenty more," he said over his shoulder.

"So we'll need another boat." That was a problem I could handle.

"I'll get the others from the kitchen and meet you out front." Frances hurried from the room.

"What about my client?" Smith asked when we were alone.

Client. His training was showing. I laughed. "You mean Amelia?"

"Yeeesss." The reply was hesitant.

For a moment we stood staring at each other in the ruined parlor. My eyes drank in his battered face, the rumpled clothes stained with blood. Now that I knew who he was, I didn't know why I hadn't recognized him immediately. Every word and action shouted his identity. The attraction we'd felt in the barn resumed with force: his and mine, our emotions twining together. The feelings rushed through me, singing in my veins and threatening to block out all rational thought.

He was still waiting for further explanation.

"That woman who was just here is Frances," I said. "Miles, I came for her because of Amelia."

Smith stared, his battered face puzzled. "You know my name."

Miles Smithson to be exact. If I hadn't already deduced it, his thoughts were practically yelling it at me now. "Yes. I also know you're an attorney with Wellison and Durham. But now it's your turn to answer a question. How did you know to come here?"

He rubbed a hand across his chin, wincing as he touched a bruise. "Amelia wrote a letter saying she was leaving Savannah to come here to free Frances and her family. She was worried about making it in time, and Alabama is closer and the mail arrived fast. I thought I might get here in time if she couldn't. I pulled a few strings so it would all be legal just in case Johansson had fake papers."

I *had* told Miles about Frances in my last letter, written and mailed on the trail to Mississippi. I knew he would share my outrage, but never had I imagined that he would abandon his busy practice to travel here to help me.

"I knew where she stayed the last time she was here . . ." he began again, and then stopped. "Wait, are you with her? Is she at the hotel?"

I heard the hope and understood that despite his

attraction for me, he'd give me up forever if that was the only way he could meet Amelia. She meant a lot to him. More than she should. Knowing this made me want to tell him what his letters had meant to an old lady who wasn't really old at all.

"She'll be on the boat." What else could I say? He wouldn't understand if I said that Amelia Mitchell was the name I'd made up for him and his siblings, an alias like a dozen others I'd used over the past century.

"So what is your real name?"

"Ava O'Hare."

He stared. "O'Hare. You're related to Amelia then. O'Hare was her mother's maiden name."

"Something like that."

"No wonder you seem so familiar." He closed the space between us with several long strides. "Wait. The cut on your face, from your fight with Cardiff. It's healing."

I nodded. "It is."

He studied me for a long moment, again waiting. He did that well—waiting. I could feel Ritter's impatience outside the front door. He should have left already to retrieve Johansson's papers, but I'd never get him to leave me alone with an unknown, not after what had happened tonight.

"There isn't time for that conversation," I said. "Are you coming with us to the boat?"

"Absolutely. This has been the most fun I've had since law school."

I knew it wasn't really for me that he was coming, but

for Amelia, and that only added to my anticipation. "If this is fun, you're as crazy as I am."

He smiled. "No one is that crazy."

He hadn't met Locke yet or the rest of the Renegades.

I turned to go, but his hand grabbed mine. "Is there time for this? Because I've been waiting it seems my whole life." He leaned forward and kissed me.

I'd been waiting a lot longer. He'd taken years to become the man whose letters had first intrigued and then called to me. I kissed him back, opening my mind and letting some of the emotion run back to him. He wouldn't understand what it was, but it might get his mind off the other me that he couldn't wait to meet.

"There's always time for this," I said.

PART FOUR

Present Day - Kansas City, Kansas

The Greatest Revenge

CHAPTER 12

"MILES STAYED EVEN AFTER LEARNING THE TRUTH," I TOLD Erin Radkey in the hospital cafeteria, rubbing my finger against an ice-cold glass of lemonade. "We were married in less than a week, and he worked with us after that. Well, Locke went back to England to be with her son and to keep an eye on their descendants, but Ritter and I stayed, and our little band of Renegades grew. Ritter also kept track of Johansson until he was killed in a logging accident a few years later. Not long after, we began patrolling the West Coast as the territories were organized. We lost a lot of good people, but we did a lot of good and kept the Emporium from taking over the States."

"I wish I could have met Miles." Erin put her elbows on the table and leaned forward. Her hair, once burned to stubble, was several inches long now. Only a week had passed since her Change, and I claimed three centuries, but we looked more like sisters than women separated by four generations. In actuality, Erin was my fourth great-granddaughter.

"I wish you could have met him too."

Erin was silent for a long moment. "Do you miss him?"

My heart squeezed just a little when she asked. Miles was the first man I'd loved as a wife, but not the last. I'd outlived several mortal spouses and given birth to half a dozen children. Despite how hard it always was to lose them, I wasn't against loving again. "I will always miss him, but we had a good life, and our posterity"—I reached across the table and took her hand—"has made me proud."

It had been too long since someone in my family line had Changed, and Erin and her younger brother, Jace, had given me new purpose. I believed Erin's sensing ability would far outreach my own, and her dedication to her duty as a guardian of humanity would do more to help our cause than anything else we'd done in the past century. Jace would need a lot more experience before he'd come into his full usefulness as a combat Unbounded, but that he'd Changed at all bordered on miraculous. I felt rich with their presence. Even Chris, their older mortal brother, had joined our Renegade cell, bringing his two motherless children with him. We would have to bury them long before we were ready to let them go, but they made the battle worth fighting.

Erin took a long pull of her lemonade; I hadn't yet

been able to teach her that it was best sipped. "You've done it then," she said.

"What's that?"

"When Chris told me his wife had been murdered by the Emporium, I told him the greatest revenge we have is to go about our lives, raising our children, and finding happiness wherever we can." Erin's gray eyes held mine. "Ava, you've done that. Gabriel is gone, and so are Miles and your children, but you went on, found a life, and you were happy." Her smile faltered. "For a while, after we almost lost everyone, I didn't really believe it was possible to be happy while the Emporium exists, but now with Ritter—"

She didn't have to say more. I understood. She had hope. "He's different now," I told her.

Erin smiled a secret smile that told me something had passed between them. Maybe something good. But I'd have to wait to find out because Ritter was on his way now to our location. I wondered if she felt him yet, or if she needed more time to develop her new ability.

Ritter strode into the nearly deserted cafeteria, followed by our Unbounded healer Dimitri Sidorov, who was as close to a co-leader as I'd ever had. He'd been alive for a thousand years, and we'd been working together well over a century. Shorter than Ritter by a head, he was every bit as wide, and he exuded an almost animal attractiveness.

He could kill or heal with a touch, but he was also one of the kindest men I'd ever known.

"The room is ready," Dimitri said. "They will begin to prepare your father as soon as your operation is underway."

Erin's momentary surprise at seeing them told me she had been concentrating too hard on me to sense them coming. She jumped to her feet, her lemonade forgotten. "I'm ready." After a bloody clash with the Emporium, her father needed a heart, and she was determined to be the donor. Only one focus point, so she'd survive and generate a new one. I couldn't blame her for wanting to save his life.

Ritter stepped closer to Erin, though they didn't touch, and emotion between them flared, too strong for their mental shields to hide altogether. Ritter was still a killing machine and the best tactical leader I'd ever worked with, but Erin had turned his life upside down this past week. I believed he'd finally found what I'd wanted for him, something more than revenge to live for. I knew that frightened him even more than he hated the Emporium, but it was a risk he took because he loved my granddaughter.

Together they strode toward the doorway. Ritter was showing Erin a new pistol he'd arranged for her, the gift a mating ritual understood only by combat Unbounded and tolerated by the rest of us. Erin didn't yet have a clue; she'd think the weapon came from our general arsenal.

She also didn't know, and he'd never think to tell her, that it was a temporary goodbye, a placeholder until he returned from London. No way was I getting in the middle of that. They would have to work it out for themselves.

As we followed them, Dimitri's hand brushed mine. I met his dark eyes, my breath catching in my throat. He was my best friend, and it had been a long time since I'd felt that way about a man, the first time for a man who was also Unbounded.

Soon I would have a decision to make.

Maybe it was time for a little more of the living kind of revenge.

THE END

Teyla Branton grew up avidly reading science fiction and fantasy and watching Star Trek reruns with her large family. They lived on a little farm where she loved to visit the solitary cow and collect (and juggle) the eggs, usually making it back to the house with most of them intact. On that same farm she once owned thirty-three gerbils and eighteen cats, not a good mix, as it turns out. Teyla always had her nose in a book and daydreamed about someday creating her own worlds.

Teyla is now married, mostly grown up, and has seven kids, so life at her house can be very interesting (and loud), but writing keeps her sane. She thrives on the energy and daily amusement offered by her children, the semi-ordered chaos giving her a constant source of writing material. Grabbing any snatch of free time from her hectic life, Teyla writes novels, often with a child on her lap. She warns her children that if they don't behave, they just might find themselves in her next book!

She's been known to wear pajamas all day when working on a deadline, and is often distracted enough to burn dinner. (Okay, pretty much 90% of the time.) A sign on her office door reads: DANGER. WRITER AT WORK. ENTER AT YOUR OWN RISK.

She loves writing fiction and traveling, and she hopes to write and travel a lot more. She also loves shooting guns, martial arts, and belly dancing. She has worked in the publishing business for over twenty years. Teyla also writes romance and suspense under the name Rachel Branton. For more information, please visit http://www.TeylaBranton.com.

Made in the USA
Columbia, SC
17 May 2022